Cal Restrepo, victim of a road rage automobile accident, emerges from unconsciousness into a world he does not recognize.

Under the care of the doctors at Wending Hills and the help of his friends and neighbors, Cal gradually recovers his memory and the full use of his body. Yet, so many of the memories do not fit what he feels is the "real" Cal.

Are his memories still clouded and unreliable, or was the Cal Restrepo who existed before the accident someone entirely different than the man who survived?

I0584356

LEFT IN THE

DARK

Zev de Valera

A NineStar Press Publication

www.ninestarpress.com

Left in the Dark

Printed in the USA

ISBN: 978-1-64890-246-8

First Edition, April, 2021

Also available in eBook, ISBN: 978-1-64890-245-1

CONTENT WARNING:

Depictions of cheating by a main character; romantic intentions between an underage teen by an older acquaintance; discussion of an off-page teenage suicide; discussion and depiction of an off-page car accident; injuries sustained, including temporary amnesia; and recuperation.

Prologue

Swish-thunk.

Swish-thunk.

The sound repeats in my mind like the click of a metronome.

Played over this rhythm are screams, screeches—both human and inhuman.

The heat and the fire are unbearable, inescapable.

Then, they come.

Crawling from the churning flames of the pit like the freakish imaginings of Hieronymus Bosch.

Twisted. Grotesque.

Arms extended in impossible gestures.

Hands reaching, reaching.

Fingers grasping, beseeching.

I feel them on me; pressing.

Stop it!

One of the horrors clings to me, raises its head. From a twisted gash of a mouth come the words:

I love you.

Swish-thunk.

Swish-thunk.

Chapter One

CAL

"I'd like to keep you, but I have to let you go."

The words immediately conjured in my mind the lyrics of some old country tune. They seemed incongruous coming from the mouth of the grim-faced, matronly South Asian woman seated before me. But, then, she merely appeared forbidding and matronly. Dr. Malhotra was a sympathetic person, and it was only her professional garb and tightly chignoned hair that gave a suggestion of the matron. Still, I found it difficult to imagine her plucking at guitar strings and warbling in a sad, twangy voice.

"Rothman and his physical therapy team have given you the green light," continued Malhotra, "so there is no reason for continuing your—"

"Imprisonment?"

"For continuing your *stay* at Wending Hills."

"But?"

Dr. Malhotra removed her glasses. After closing the file that lay on her desk, she folded her hands over it and addressed me with an earnest expression. A classic physician's pose—almost a parody.

I'm not a doctor, but I play one on television.

"I realize that asking you to reconsider staying on is a waste of time," Malhotra continued. I nodded agreement. "However, I can—and must—insist on a period of home care."

"*Home* care?"

I imagined myself as a frail old man accepting soupçons of saliva-laced gruel from a sadistic nurse.

"Yes. Just for a few weeks. To ensure that you're not experiencing any unanticipated cognitive impairment and to continue your physical therapy. POW will send someone to your home tomorrow morning."

"POW?"

"Practitioners on Wheels. They do excellent work."

I sighed, accepting defeat. I trusted Malhotra—though I'd always argued with her on principle.

"Whatever you say, Doc."

Malhotra's eyes narrowed. "I'm not sure I'm convinced by this sudden acquiescence, but I'll take it."

"So, I'm officially sprung?"

"Yes. A pity you don't have an orange jumpsuit to take with you as a memento."

"Funny."

I pushed myself up from the chair, feeling suddenly awkward. Like a kid saying goodbye to his mother as he set off for college. Happy, excited, nervous and sad all at the same time. Malhotra stood and pulled a business card from her lab coat.

"Please keep in touch, Cal," she said, handing me the card. "My mobile number is on the back. Let me know how you're getting on."

I tucked the card into the pocket of my chinos, accepting this as a gesture of friendship. The visiting nurse would keep Malhotra apprised of my progress. There was no need for the extra effort.

"Of course. Thank you, Dr. Malhotra."

I hoped I would never speak to her again.

I smiled, she smiled, and I turned to walk to the door, leaning heavily on my cane. I depressed the lever and pushed.

"Cal."

"Yes?" I asked, looking over my shoulder.

"You're going to be all right."

I passed into the hallway and closed the door carefully behind me.

All right.

I was going to be all right.

Sure.

I'd spent more than a month in physical therapy, recovering the use of my battered body, and an equal amount of time with Malhotra, striving to recover my memory and work through the issues of a near-death experience and survivor guilt.

All right.

A relative term.

*

Wending Hills.

The name had that ring of false pastoral splendor one often associates with such establishments as if the promise of imaginary bucolic vistas might soften the blow of infirmity. Wending Hills, however, lived up to its name. Situated just north of Peekskill, New York, on a high promontory overlooking the Hudson, my room in the sanatorium provided a clear view to the hills and valleys that sloped elegantly toward the river. Now, in early summer, the verdure was an undulating, multitextured carpet under a gentle breeze. From the small balcony of my cell—one of the more spacious suites allotted to those deemed free of suicidal tendencies—I could just about glimpse the grounds of the Rockefeller Kykuit estate.

Glancing through the brochure that I'd never bothered to look at before, I discovered that Wending Hills was built around the same time as the famous industrialist's compound and was designed by a student of Rockefeller's architect. Originally a spa retreat, Wending Hills had adopted many identities over the years: a military headquarters, a children's hospital, a senior care campus. Now, it was a church-affiliated facility that specialized in physical therapy and the treatment of PTSD and memory loss.

I turned my thoughts away from the history of Wending Hills and toward my own. Out there, northeast along I-95, lay the home in which I'd spent the last two years of my life. When I tried to look back further—to my childhood, for instance—memories became frustrating chimeras. I recalled my father and mother clearly but only in disjointed snippets, brief but vivid flashbacks. Malhotra had assured me this was merely a temporary aberration, that eventually I should recover enough of the knowledge of my past to be on par with the average person of middle age. Or even have an advantage.

"Advantage?"

"Yes, Cal. Our memories are colored by experience. We see our younger selves as a reflection of the person we are now, who we've become. You, on the other hand, could view past events with unique clarity, unencumbered by the influence of recent life events. Also, you must understand that much of what we consider 'memories' of our early lives are, in fact, nothing of the kind."

"What?"

Malhotra laughed. A little huff that seemed to brush aside my ignorance with professional magnanimity.

"We hear our parents or other family members speak of events, behaviors from our childhood. You know the sort of thing: 'Oh, I'll never forget how Suzie loved her first puppy' or 'Timmy was always such a curious child,' or 'Don't you remember when...?' Of course, we don't remember, but we accept these third-party references as truth, indistinguishable from our real memories. As we grow older, this process becomes subtler, more complex as our desire to create our own reality shapes our opinions of our actions and their consequences.

"What I mean is that you may very well see your real past. Unfiltered, objective. As if you were watching an unbiased biography of yourself. Don't think of your condition as an entirely negative experience. Rather, look upon it as a chance to begin anew, to grow in ways that perhaps you may not have done otherwise."

"Look on the bright side, in other words?"

Malhotra sighed and shrugged her shoulders.

"Simple, but accurate."

"I'll send you my bill."

Though I made light of them, Malhotra's words disturbed me. I'd never thought of memory as something inherently deceptive. I'd never thought about it at all. She'd meant to reassure me, but Malhotra had accomplished the opposite. Her psychobabble had only increased my anxiety.

I finished stuffing my few belongings into the duffel I'd purchased on a whim at the institution's café/bookshop. It was black, ugly, and emblazoned with the cartoonish Wending Hills logo of mountains and a rising sun, reminding me of a raisin box.

Why did I remember *that*?

I don't even like raisins.

Funny how I seem to recall the things I dislike with such amazing clarity. Raisins, obviously. And Habit Rouge, Dr. Rothman's scent of choice. I always thought doctors were prohibited from wearing artificial fragrances, and I took an instant, irrational dislike to Rothman the moment I first smelled him. Unfortunately, Habit Rouge had also been Paul's favorite scent.

Paul.

More unpleasant memories. The bastard was going to leave me to become some sort of lay monk. He hadn't been planning to leave me for another man, he'd been planning to leave me for *the* other man. The Son of God. I suppose if I were a different kind of person, I might have felt some bizarre sort of comfort in this. What I felt was anger. Fuck-you-you-asshole kind of anger.

"It's not you, Cal. It's me."

Paul had insisted in that newfound, gentle, and oh-so-irritating cleric-to-be voice.

"Fuck you!"

I should have seen it coming, and I didn't. Or I refused to see. According to Malhotra, the anger was with myself more than with Paul. I was projecting. Maybe she was right. But I found it difficult to accept any culpability in the dissolution of my relationship with Paul. He was the one who had withheld sexual intimacy, he was the one who'd distanced himself with his ever-growing religious obsession.

"And how did that make you feel?"

One of Malhotra's favorite questions.

"Like shit. What do you think?"

I zipped the duffel and took one last look at the view.

A minivan waited downstairs to take me to the Metro North station. As I turned from the window, one of those memory flashes hit, unexpected, clear, and poignant.

"Why do they call it a 'variety pack'? There's only four of them. Not much choice."

I say this with a sour face as my mother slaps the carton of miniature cereal boxes in front of me and then turns to tend to the opening of her carton of Marlboros.

"I have no idea, little man. Just pick one and eat. You're already late for school. And I'll be late for work if we don't put a wiggle in it."

I watch her as she lights her cigarette from the gas burner, then leans against the breakfast counter, her geometric print wrap dress juxtaposed in all its polyester glory to the backdrop of avocado-green appliances.

"Love Will Keep Us Together" starts to play on the clock radio, the digital readout blinking 12:00 as it has done since it was installed the year before.

My mother groans.

"That song again?"

"I like it," I say as I punch the perforated opening in the tiny box of Frosted Flakes in time with the tune.

My mother ignores my comment. "Did you finish your homework?"

"Of course."

She appraises me with a squint-eyed look. I proceed to munch on cereal, my face a mask of false virtue.

My mother takes another drag, then laughs.

"You know, kid, you really ought to go into politics. You're a natural."

I didn't go into politics, though I might have been a natural fabulist. Instead, I became a costume designer. I suppose the two fields of work have something in common: the practitioners of each make their livings by contributing to the creation of fantasy worlds.

And wasn't that where I found myself? In a world I understood but did not entirely appreciate for all its permutations and layers? That was the problem, as I saw it. Malhotra had tried to put a good spin on it—that was her job, after all—but her idea that I would have a unique and clear perspective on my past was lost on me. I did not want a unique and clear perspective.

I wanted *my* perspective, goddammit.

And it was there. But only in frustrating, often unrelated bits.

How long do I have to wait until my mental kaleidoscope shifts and I feel whole again?

Maudlin thoughts about the state of my memory were summarily shelved as I attempted to stand without the aid of the accursed three-pronged cane.

Shit!

Shooting pain ran though my back and legs, then eased as I righted myself and stood straight. Getting up and down was agony—and would be for some weeks to come, according to Dr. Habit Rouge's physical therapy entourage.

Thoughts of Paul again.

Get out of my mind, you bastard.

Then, Malhotra's voice, both low and strident, an Indian Margaret Thatcher:

"You need to move away from demonizing Paul and allow yourself to grieve for him. Paul shook up your life, took something you saw as an absolute, and showed you that it wasn't. It was hard to suddenly realize he no longer needed you in his life the way you needed or wanted him. Now, he's gone forever. Holding on to the old anger will only hinder you in your future life."

"This is all his fault," I murmured as I clutched the arms of my chair, not really believing the words as I said them but wanting to. Oh, how I wanted to.

"*Paul did not cause your accident. Your understandably emotional reaction to what you viewed as his abandonment of you may have caused you to behave in a less than cautious manner—*"

"What?? Now you're saying the accident was my fault? I was sideswiped by a drunk driver, for Christ's sake!"

"*There are those who believe that everything that happens to us is, in one way or another, our own fault.*"

"Bullshit."

Malhotra eyed me for a moment, then said, "Would you have been driving over the speed limit under normal circumstances?"

I shrugged.

"*If you hadn't been doing so, would the accident still have happened?*"

"Bullshit."

It was the best I could come up with. I didn't want to deal with Malhotra's ugly truths. I saw the trap she'd set. Admitting to even a tangential culpability in the circumstances of the accident smoothly set me up for an admission of my part in the collapse of my relationship with Paul.

"*I know you understand, Cal,*" *said Malhotra. "The thing is, I want you to know you understand.*"

*

The taxi smelled faintly of cannabis—a gift from the last fare, I supposed. Or maybe it was the driver who had indulged. He certainly fit a certain stereotype: Guns and

Roses T-shirt, a well-worn baseball cap with a Confederate flag sewn on it, an anemic pallor and a skinny body to go with it. His blue eyes, though, were clear and quite beautiful.

"Where've you been, buddy?" the driver asked.

He knows me?

He watched me struggle with my duffel and my cane as I hobbled into his vehicle, and I was tempted to say that I'd been on vacation in Fiji.

"I've been in the hospital."

"Damn, man. Bummer."

"Yeah. Major bummer."

"Thought you moved or something."

I wondered briefly what "or something" might be. Kidnapping? Murder? Then, I gave him my address.

He laughed. "Hey, my mem'ry ain't that fucked up, man! Only been what? A month or so?"

I managed a smile. He couldn't know. But his reference to a fucked-up memory hurt like hell.

As we covered the short distance from the train station to my house, I eyed the passing scenery with increasing anxiety. To my relief, it was all familiar. Yet, it was like that dreamy reality I often experienced after returning home from an extended vacation in an exotic land. As if I really *had* gone to Fiji. And I had this creeping dread that my grip on reality would suddenly snap, and I would revert to the terrified man with no memory whom I'd been for the first week following the accident.

"Home sweet home, buddy," said the driver with an encouraging note of conviction as he rolled up the driveway of my house.

It was a charming house. A renovated twenties cottage. Just large enough for a husband, a wife, and two children. Or a gay couple with a dog.

Bruno!

I finally remembered Bruno.

I was smiling like a doofus as I paid the driver. This sudden little burst of knowledge both pleased and relieved me immensely.

"Your change," the driver said, stretching out a cadaverous arm.

"Oh, um...keep it."

I was overtipping, but I was feeling magnanimous. Share the joy, and all that.

"Thanks, man. Appreciate it. You got my number. Any time you need a ride, just gimme a call."

"Thanks."

With that, he reversed out of the driveway and sped off.

I had no idea what his number was.

*

I looked the house over, then shuffled around the front garden. Everything had been well tended in my absence. That was down to my old friend, Joshua, who'd also been looking after my newly remembered dog. He'd contracted an excellent maintenance service. I glanced at my watch. Joshua was due to arrive soon, Bruno in tow.

"He'll be the best memory trigger," Joshua had said during his last visit to Wending Hills. "Unless, of course, you're faking it. Then, he'll growl at you, and I'll know right away that you're actually Cal's long-lost evil twin."

I laughed, another memory clicking into place. Joshua could always make me laugh.

"So, what happened to the real Cal?"

"They're both *real*, you idiot. I said 'twin' not 'impostor.' Pay attention."

Joshua was an opera singer. Ridiculous plots were his stock in trade.

"Let's see. Yes. He follows you. He'd been stalking you for months, seething with jealously after having escaped from the mental hospital to which he (falsely, of course) believes you had him forcibly committed. He witnesses your car go over the cliff—"

"There was no cliff. It was a verge."

"Whatever. Evil Cal crashes his own car and gets pretty banged up, but he must take the risk to pull off his scheme. Poor Paul, beyond hope, cannot bear witness to his evil act. Of course, despite his injuries, Evil Cal still has enough strength to haul Good Cal's lifeless body from the car, switch clothing, wallets and mobile phones, and bury the corpse in the verge thingy. Oh, and break his own leg to further divert suspicion."

"All while singing the big Act One aria."

"*Certamente.*"

Well, Joshua was probably right about Bruno; my dog's presence might well lead to more lightbulb moments. I found that I was starting to feel tentatively hopeful. Or less hopeless, at any rate.

The sound of exuberant barking heralded the approach of my friend and my pet. I glanced up from my study of a rhododendron to see Joshua's red Mini pull up the driveway and watched, amused, as Bruno attempted to clamber over my friend and leap through the window while Joshua fought to extricate himself from his seatbelt.

"Get down, you silly animal! *I* can't wait to get away from *you* either."

"Easy, boy," I said, leaning heavily on my cane as I approached the car. I opened the door for Joshua, and Bruno was on me in a bound, whining, barking, wiggling, and sniffing.

"And Timmy and Lassie are reunited at last!" Joshua declared with a dramatic arm wave as he emerged from the vehicle.

"Thank you," I said, playing with Bruno's fuzzy, triangular black ears—a mark of his chow-shepherd mix.

"I don't know why you insisted on taking the train, Cal. We could have swung by Bedlam and brought you home in style."

In style, indeed. I checked out Joshua's gear, his costume for this outing: a Madison Avenue boutique version of English country squire tweeds. His medium-length, coffee-brown hair was carefully disheveled, and he'd allowed a few gray strands to shine through, complementing the wiry silver in his neatly trimmed beard. He was a handsome man of the burly type—a look particularly suited to the baritone roles he sang.

"Go on and play with your beastie while I get my bag and provisions."

"Provisions?"

"Food. And champagne, of course, darling. You know, welcome home, here's to you, etcetera, etcetera."

"I can't drink. I'm on pain meds."

"Meds, schmeds. Skip a dose. The bubbly will do you more good. Plus, you'll need something to wash down the escargot and the coquille Saint Jacques."

Real food, not the Wending Hills special of mixed steamed vegetables and some version of overcooked chicken.

"You're a treasure, Joshua."

"I know. I can't help myself."

I felt something stir within me then, with Bruno licking my hand and Joshua beaming jovially. The frustration and anger of the past weeks receded somewhat, and a small but strong fire of optimism began to burn. My life wasn't over. Malhotra was correct. I was going to be all right.

Joshua embraced me; Bruno danced around us. Things were looking up.

*

We dined alfresco. Joshua prepared the meal utilizing the neglected summer kitchen on the backyard deck. It had been used all of two times since its installation. Paul had insisted that it would add value to the property. I couldn't see the appeal of cooking outdoors in the heat of summer when one had a state-of-the-art kitchen inside a temperature-controlled home.

Joshua proved the correctness of Paul's decision though. It was a beautiful evening, neither hot nor cool, and a gentle breeze mixed the smells of herbs and spices with the scents of my extensive rose garden.

"Are you sure I can't help you?" I called out across the yard from the comfort of the swing nestled beneath an oak tree. Bruno lay on top of me, snoring softly.

"Darling, you once rang me up to ask if you could microwave a packaged cake mix. Does that answer your question?"

Well, it *was* a rhetorical question. I sipped my champagne and prodded the swing into motion with my good leg. It was getting on eight o'clock, and the sky was taking on a spectacular presunset glow. I stroked Bruno's fur and observed Joshua's Kitchen Stadium performance. It was a life-is-good moment.

"*Tutti a tavola!*"

Obeying Joshua's summons, I limped my way to the house.

We sat at the mission-style table in the sunroom adjacent to the outdoor kitchen. The escargots and scallops were delicious, and I was feeling inebriated on two glasses of champagne and an unquantifiable amount of goodwill. I smiled as Joshua refilled our flutes.

"Are you trying to get me drunk and take advantage of me?" I asked.

Joshua threw me one of his broad, pantomime looks that could only have been believable if viewed from the other side of the orchestra pit. We both laughed at a long-standing joke between us. In the early days of our friendship, we'd occasionally masturbated together. Our one and only foray into sexual intercourse—Joshua called it "bumping pussies"—had ended in giggles and was followed by a companionable night of eating popcorn, watching a minimarathon of Absolutely Fabulous, and getting drunk.

I reached out and covered Joshua's left hand with my right.

"Thank you for today."

Joshua shrugged. "I've missed you. And it gave me a good excuse to miss rehearsals."

I knew he wasn't exaggerating; opera rehearsals were long and grueling. Joshua Summerly was infamously "temperamental" but tolerated by directors and managers because of his beautiful vocal instrument, exceptional acting ability, and handsome face. He sold tickets. The occasional truancy was met with a sigh and an eye roll.

"*Trovatore*?"

I'd perused the season catalogue from the Met.

"Yes. Not one of my favorites, as you know, but a crowd-pleaser."

"It didn't please *me*," I replied. "I fell asleep the first time I saw it. *You* were wonderful, of course."

"Of course. I'm glad you remember." Joshua gave me a searching look. "About your memory..."

"Yes?"

"Well...what's it like now? Your condition, I mean."

"Weird." I sipped more Veuve Clicquot. "The distant past is a jumble—there's total clarity as well as black holes. I remember my first dog, King, back when I was five. I recall events from my early childhood clearly, yet my high school and college years are a blur. It's like...I know who I am, but not always who I *was*. Does that make any sense? On the other hand, a few months of my life before the accident are almost a complete blank."

I studied the bubbles in my flute and looked up at Joshua's kindly, worried expression.

"Dr. Habit Rouge—"

"Who?"

"The neurologist. He says my noggin's fine. Just a matter of time for everything to shift back into place. But Malhotra's diagnosis is another story."

"Ah, the shrink," Joshua murmured. "I thought she was a tad cagey. And she treated me more like another patient than your friend. I suppose it's her brief—to always see monsters under the bed."

"You? A monster?"

"No. I mean, she told me to tread lightly. She warned me that pushing too hard to help you remember might have the opposite effect. And the stress might cause you to become...disturbed."

I looked away. Played with Bruno's ruff.

"So, I'm officially a nutjob?"

Joshua cursed. "Come on, Cal. She never said anything of the kind. But I *have* read about cases like yours."

"I'm a *case* now." I swilled the rest of my champagne. "Don't worry, Joshua. I'm not going to go berserk and chop you into pieces and bury you under the rose bushes."

"Don't be absurd. I'm talking about PTSD and that sort of thing."

"I know. Malhotra believes my 'condition' is a combination of retrograde amnesia caused by head trauma and a mental block of recent memories resulting from my emotional state at the time of the accident. But that doesn't add up, does it? I mean, I remember Paul, our life together, that final argument." I'd yet to recall the specifics of the crash and hoped I never would. "So, why can't I remember everything that happened a few months *before* all that? What could I be subconsciously repressing?"

Joshua's expression was pensive as he said, "That's what Dr. M. suggests? That you don't *want* to remember?

"Um-hum."

Joshua considered this for a moment, then shrugged his shoulders.

"Just forget about it, then."

"I already have, Joshua. That's the problem."

"No. I mean, don't try to remember." Joshua glanced down at Bruno. "Let sleeping dogs lie, as it were. The doctor advised me not to pressure you—so, don't pressure yourself. If it is something important, it will most likely come back to you. And it may very well turn out that that blank space has a purely physical cause."

"True. It's not as though I murdered someone or robbed a bank."

"Or both," suggested Joshua.

I responded by throwing a piece of baguette at him.

"I ought," I continued, "to concentrate on getting my body back into shape and let the rest take its course. That reminds me, the visiting nurse is due tomorrow morning. That should be a real joy."

"Expecting Nurse Ratched?"

I smiled. "Or Diesel."

"Good luck. I'm afraid I must shove off quite early in the morning, so I'll miss the show. But do call me and give me all the gruesome details."

We talked a while longer, mostly about work and the doings of mutual friends, many of whom I struggled to remember. Mentally and physically worn out, I began to fade as evening surrendered to night.

"I think it's time for sleepy bye," I said.

"Be off with ye, then," replied Joshua, shooing me with his napkin. "I'll clean up and take the animal for his postprandial stroll."

"Thank you."

I heaved myself up, flinched at the stiffness and pain in my legs and back, then gripped my cane and commenced my exit. As I paused to give Joshua a peck on the cheek, I noted the look of distaste with which he favored my pharmacy-issue walking aide.

"That's not *you* at all," Joshua said. "Not to worry though. Your fairy godbrother has it well in hand."

"What are you talking about, Joshua?"

"You'll see. In the meantime, are you sure you don't need help?"

"I'll be fine," I lied. "See you in the morning."

*

I took the first-floor guest bedroom, and Joshua accepted the minor luxury of the master suite in the converted attic. I argued, logically, that the daybed in my workroom was too small for someone of Joshua's proportions and that the slog up the stairs would be too strenuous for someone in my condition. In truth, had I desired to sleep in my own bed, I could probably have dragged myself the short distance and then collapsed painfully and gratefully atop the feathered duvet. But the last thing I wanted was to face that king-sized testament to my ruined relationship.

My housekeeper had been in the day before to "open the house"—as the antiquated saying goes—and all was perfectly cleaned, polished, and arranged. Staged. Ready for a television real estate show. I would have preferred to have found the place in the unkempt state in which I'd most likely left it. That would have been more realistic. More welcoming. The five-star turndown made me feel as much a stranger in my home as I felt in my head.

I lay awake, the guest room proving to be no escape from poignant memories. Paul and I had shopped together for each item of furniture and décor. We had argued over wallpaper versus paint. We'd made love on the hardwood floor that we'd stripped and refinished—trying unsuccessfully to revive some of the passion of our early years together. I tried to push these thoughts away, then laughed aloud at the irony. I was suffering from amnesia yet had the strongest desire to forget.

"You're an asshole," I mumbled to myself as I punched a pillow and fought back tears. Then, the sound of a soft, sad whine pulled me from the brink of self-pity. I sat up. Bruno lay in front of the open doorway, head on paws. We'd trained him never to enter the guest room, and the fact that I was now sleeping in it must have been agonizing for the poor devil. Bruno had always slept on or near our bed, despite Paul's protests. I suddenly realized I'd not considered the animal's feelings. First Paul's departure, then my absence. Bruno was doubtless scared and confused.

"Come here, sweetie." I patted the side of the bed in invitation. Bruno whined a little more and made a sort of huff, clearly struggling between training and desire. "It's okay," I continued, "Paul's not around to whack you on the rump with a newspaper." Bruno wiggled, and his tail began to swish. I thought he understood me. I tapped the bed again, smiling. "Come on, you goofy mongrel." Finally, Bruno stood up and took a few cautious steps, then leaped the remainder of the distance to the bed. He rooted around gleefully for a bit before taking his accustomed place near my feet.

Comforted by the dog's affection, I began to doze. Then, to the rhythm of Bruno's breathing, I fell into the deepest sleep I'd experienced in months.

*

Joshua was gone when I woke up. True to his natural thoughtfulness, he'd left the coffee set up and ready to brew. Taped to the machine was a note. I pressed the start button and unfolded the note.

Look on the dining room table

Curious, I moved to the other side of the kitchen and looked through the arched passage into the dining room. At the center of the round rosewood table was a large arrangement of hydrangeas, next to which lay an oblong box wrapped in Christmas-themed paper. I waited impatiently as the coffee began to brew, then poured myself a small, premature cup of java and limped my way to the dining room.

The package wasn't much of a puzzle, judging by its shape, too narrow for flowers and frighteningly long for a sex toy. Recalling Joshua's promise to rectify my cane situation, I eagerly ripped open both paper and box. I could imagine Joshua, who opened gifts with a surgeon's precision, shaking his head at my childlike abandon. Within the cardboard box lay another box resting upon a bed of tissue paper. It was veneered with what appeared to be leather and gilded in the style of a jewelry case. I removed the box, set it on the table, and proceeded to lift the delicate gold clasp. The lid sprang back to reveal an exquisite mahogany opera cane with a silver, L-shaped handle, the tip fashioned in the likeness of a wolf's head. There was another note taped to the cane.

The only good thing—other than my reputation— to survive that ill-fated Seattle production of Dracula.

I smiled, relieved that I understood Joshua's reference. Indeed, I recalled a snippet of rare praise from the generally scathing reviews of Joshua's first and last foray into nonoperatic musical theater:

It was Mr. Summerly's nuanced interpretation of the titular character—which he seemed to pull from the ether, rather than from the hackneyed book—and his masterly navigation of the complex score that kept the audience in their seats for the first act and brought them back for the next two. Absent Summerly's bravura performance, the show ought to be stabbed through the heart and sealed in a crypt for eternity.

The walking stick was beautifully made, and it felt good in my hand. Apparently, Joshua had had it resized to suit my lesser height. It took but a few experimental turns around the dining room for me to decide that it was perfect and that the three-pronged institutional number was history. True, the stage prop may not have been as supportive, but its style lent me a sense of confidence I'd lacked, a desire to swagger rather than shuffle. I imagined myself as the dashing, handsome Dracula of stage and screen—not the ancient ghoul of the novel—with the power to seduce unsuspecting young men with a mesmeric gaze.

I was enjoying this daydream when the doorbell rang.

Damn. The nurse.

Traversing the distance from the dining room to the foyer took a bit of steam from my newfound confidence, but I was still feeling upbeat when I opened the front door.

And then...

"Good morning. Mr. Restrepo? I'm Nurse Practitioner Marc Duguay."

I stood there like a moron, feeling every one of my fifty-two years and the weight of my infirmity as I stared at the earnestly smiling, handsome millennial in chinos, polo shirt, and lab coat. He extended one hand in greeting and held up his credentials, which hung from a lanyard around his neck, with the other.

I blinked.

"*¿Habla usted español?*"

He asked, his brow wrinkling. He appeared both eager and uncertain—as if he thought he'd made a mistake but decided to make the best of it, brazen it out.

"Huh?" I asked.

Finally, I snapped out of my daze. "No. Sorry."

I met his extended hand with my own. His grip was firm and warm, his skin soft.

"Cal Restrepo," I said, trying to sound hearty. "Please, come in."

"I apologize for jumping to any racial or cultural conclusions," said Nurse Practitioner Duguay as he stepped into the foyer. "For a moment, I thought you didn't understand me."

"No offense taken. I get that all the time. Because of my name, and my looks."

My dense black hair, high cheekbones, and somewhat slanted, jet-colored eyes were a dead giveaway of my indigenous ancestry.

"My father was Chilean—of Aymara descent—but my mother was Irish-American. We didn't speak much Spanish at home. I never learned it. Well, not to the point of fluency."

I stopped, on the verge of babbling.

"I see." Duguay smiled again. It seemed genuine rather than professionally put on. I'd seen enough of those recently, so I figured I was a pretty good judge. There was warmth in his eyes as well, as if he were meeting a long-lost friend. Part of his professional playbook, no doubt.

"Would you like a coffee?"

"Absolutely. It smells great." He inhaled to punctuate his words. "It's got something in it, right? Cinnamon? No, that's not it." Another sniff. "Allspice. Definitely allspice."

"Uh...yeah, that's it. Allspice. Just a hint." Honestly, I had no clue what was in the brew. It was Joshua's concoction. If it was strong, that was all that mattered to me.

I shuffled toward the kitchen, and Nurse Practitioner Duguay followed. I glanced over my shoulder and observed him studying my gait. Not my ass, my gait. And why the hell was I sexualizing this encounter? Because he was hot, of course. And I hadn't had any in a very long time. Well, at least I could still be honest with myself. To a point.

"Your motor coordination is much less impaired than I expected," Duguay said, pulling a file from his briefcase. "Cool cane, by the way."

"Thanks. Milk or sugar?"

"Black, please."

Points to Duguay for the compliment and his coffee preference.

"Have a seat." I pointed my chin in the direction of the breakfast nook.

I stole an occasional glance at Duguay as I fussed with the coffee. He paid me no mind, giving his attention first to his paperwork and then to the view out to the garden. Nervousness exacerbated my usual unease with medical practitioners. Duguay's attractiveness—longish, curly brown surfer hair, with subtle lights only nature can bestow, delicately lashed hazel eyes, a face with chiseled bone structure, and a wiry physique—only made it worse. His mouth was slightly turned down and would have given him a somewhat cruel look if he weren't so personable.

"You have a lovely rose garden, Mr. Restrepo. Your work?"

"Yes," I replied, pride in my gardening pulling me from thoughts of Duguay's face. "Just about the first thing we did when we moved here."

Shit!

We.

How long would it be before that "we" became "I"?

I braced myself for polite questions about living arrangements, but Duguay did not pursue the subject. Of course, he probably had all the pertinent details in his file.

"Let me help you with that," he said as I placed the two sets of cups and saucers on a wooden tray and poured out the coffee. "Clearly, you can get around quite well on your own." He moved to my side and took up the tray. "But entertaining might be a bit of a challenge for a while yet."

I appreciated his professional observations couched in social niceties. And his voice. The velvety contralto possessed a familiar yet nonspecific accent. It reminded me of the voices of actors from the '30s and '40s, well-enunciated and somewhat clipped as if he'd been professionally tutored in elocution.

"There's pandoro around here somewhere," I said. "If you'd like—"

"It's on top of the refrigerator," replied Duguay as he placed the tray on the table and resumed his seat. "I couldn't help but notice the pink Bauli box. But I'm fine with just the coffee, thank you."

"So now what?" I asked as I eased myself into the nook. "I mean, what's the procedure? The doctors at Wending Hills made it sound as if you'd be making sure I take my meds and don't fall and break something that wasn't already broken."

Duguay smiled over his coffee cup. "There is that, yes. However, I specialize in recuperative therapy, particularly for those who've suffered head trauma as well as other physical and-or neurological damage. To begin with, I'll do a visual evaluation of your physical condition and observe your speech, your mood, etcetera, looking for signs of any postdischarge neurological impairment." He took a long drink of coffee before continuing.

"Then we'll move on to physical therapy. Probably the same exercises you were doing at Wending Hills. Stretching, strength training, and so on."

"I see. So, how do I look?"

The question was out of my mouth before I realized how silly it sounded. I sipped my coffee, feeling foolish.

Duguay raised an eyebrow and gazed into my eyes for a moment. A moment longer than was perhaps professionally necessary. Or maybe it was my imagination. Probably. After all, I'd done pretty much nothing but read and daydream for the last month or so.

"Surprisingly fit, under the circumstances."

I sat up straighter. I knew that by "circumstances," Duguay was referring to the accident, but his relative youth made me acutely aware of my age, something I'd rarely given much thought to before my invalid state. I tried to pull up a preaccident image of myself—gym-toned, naturally athletic, tight in all the right places, no wrinkles to speak of (thank God for those Aymara genes)—and project that image to Duguay. I'd like to think it worked.

More daydreaming. Duguay was now busy consulting his notes.

"Your physical therapist at Wending Hills saw excellent progress in your upper-body strength," murmured Duguay. "But less in your lower extremities. For now, I'll take her at her word, and we'll concentrate on your legs. Obviously, you took very good care of your body before your accident, so you shouldn't find my regimen too grueling."

Thank you for that last bit, Nurse Practitioner Duguay. You certainly know how to stroke your clients.

"More coffee?"

"Thank you, yes," replied Duguay.

I began to haul myself up, but my nurse motioned me to stay seated.

"I'll get it. We haven't started therapy yet, so enjoy the respite."

"Somehow, I don't think this is going to be quite as easy-peasy as you make it sound."

Duguay laughed as he crossed to the counter. A throaty laugh, suppressed, muted. What would it sound like when he let it out?

He returned with the carafe.

"That all depends on you, Mr. Restrepo."

"Please, call me Cal."

"That all depends on you, Cal. And you ought to call me Marc. Nurse Practitioner Duguay is a bit of a mouthful."

Hmm...I wonder...

I scrutinized his snug chinos surreptitiously as he poured.

Nicely packed.

"Thanks."

"You're quite welcome. Do you have any other questions for me?"

Are you gay?

"Um, no. Not now."

Duguay glanced out at the backyard.

"Well, then, could we take our coffee outside? I'd love to see your specimens."

"You're into gardening?" I asked, surprised at the terminology.

"Used to be. When I lived with my folks, but I don't have time now. My parents are both keen on horticulture. They own a small garden center, actually."

Duguay stood and placed our cups and saucers on the tray. I raised myself as gracefully as possible and took a firm grip on my wolf-headed cane.

"Where did you get that?" Duguay asked, eyeing the cane. "It looks like an antique."

"It might well be an antique; I don't know. But there is a story behind it."

Duguay smiled. Teeth this time. Naturally ivory, healthy teeth, not the common bleached-white variety.

"All right, then," he said, picking up the tray. "Lead me to your garden, and you can tell me all about it."

*

"Details, darling, details. What was she like?"

For a moment, I considered fabricating a description of a large, middle-aged, buxom woman in a tight polyester uniform and white brogans. But I couldn't deceive Joshua. Besides, it was inevitable that Duguay and my old friend would meet at some point.

"He," I corrected.

"*He*?"

"Yes, he. And a very good-looking he, at that."

Joshua whistled.

"You sly dog."

"Hey, man, I didn't pick him."

"Okay. How about 'you lucky bastard'?"

I imagined Joshua lounging on a sofa in his sprawling living room, which afforded an enviable view of Central Park. Sipping a whisky, probably. Jonesing for a cigarette, certainly, the stress of rehearsals still unnerving after almost thirty years.

"Better," I allowed.

"And? Come on, Cal. I've got to be at the Met, all bright-eyed and bushy-tailed, in less than an hour. Spill."

I proceeded to describe Nurse Practitioner Duguay in the driest, most detached detail. I even provided an outline of my proposed physical therapy regime. I omitted the (perceived) flirtation over coffee and the easy conversation in the garden afterward.

Joshua wasn't buying it.

"So, in other words, you're dying to get in his pants."

"Please. I don't even know if he's gay."

"I said you're dying to get in his pants. His sexual orientation is neither here nor there."

"Your logic escapes me."

"You know damn well what I mean. And it's a good thing. It's about time you started thinking about someone other than Paul. I mean, what's the point of holding on to something negative? Even if it is just a fantasy."

I heard the tinkle of ice and a slurp.

"Anyway," continued Joshua. "You're a big boy. You won't do anything silly. I hope."

"Of course not."

"Good. Sorry to be rude, but I've got to get a move on."

"Break a leg."

"Thanks. Coming from you, that has an extra piquancy, doesn't it? Love you. Bye."

Joshua hung up before I could return the endearment.

*

I spent the remainder of the afternoon and most of the evening going from room to room, poking through drawers and closets, picking up and putting down bric-a-brac. Paul had cleared out all his personal effects long ago, but those "we" objects—stuff picked up on trips, gifts from mutual friends—were everywhere. These things belonged neither to me nor Paul, but to the couple we no longer were. I vowed to rid myself of the lot. Immediately.

Easier said than done. Storage boxes and packing materials were kept in the basement, a poorly lit space at the end of an old and rickety flight of stairs. I contemplated the journey briefly, with my hand on the doorknob, then decided it was a truly dumbass idea. I imagined the headline. Horror in Hollyford: *Fifty-two-year-old retiree found dead in basement by caregiver. Caregiver held for questioning.* I was not, strictly speaking, retired, but I thought the wording had the piteous ring that newspaper writers love.

I was about to give up on my packing project when I recalled I had a few plastic file bins in the closet of my workroom. Those would do for the stuff I intended to donate to Housing Works or Goodwill. The rest could go into garbage bags. A wave of apprehension passed over me as I took in my little domain. If I'd anticipated an explosion of suppressed memories, I was disappointed. I examined the drafting table, the desk with its array of brushes and pencils stored in coffee cans, the blue tackle box, the sketchbooks and watercolor blocks. Everything perfectly familiar, and utterly mute. Oh, well. At least I could remove my extended hiatus from paid work from the list of potential causes of my memory lapse. Besides, I was meant to be taking Joshua's advice and forget about forgetting.

I collected three boxes, lugged them along to the dining room table, and began my work in earnest. While it lacked the cathartic rush I expected, the process did provide a long overdue sense of closure—the beginning of it anyway. By the time I'd scrounged some labels from the pantry, marked them up, and slapped them on, I felt the satisfaction of a mission accomplished.

Not having taken my pain medication since leaving Wending Hills, I concluded I felt better without it. I still had difficulty rotating my neck, and sitting and standing were still a challenge, my back delivering a nasty stab of pain if I moved the wrong way. My head, however, felt clearer, my mind more alert. They'd also given me a pill to help alleviate confusion, but when I read the list of side effects, I chose a little confusion as the lesser of many evils.

Happy with my self-unprescribing and proud of my first step in tchotchke disposal, I decided to celebrate with a cocktail. I mixed a gin and tonic and nursed it, leaning on the kitchen island, flipping through a cookbook. According to my American Express statements, I'd lived on food from Fresh Direct (calorie-laden prepared meals, most likely) from the time of Paul's departure until my stint at Wending Hills. But the weight I'd gained had been lost, and then some, by the subsequent institutional diet.

Since I had nothing much else to do, I thought I might finally teach myself how to cook. Paul's haute cuisine tomes were gone, not that I could have tackled them if they remained, so I'd asked Joshua to bring me something easy. Nigella Lawson's breezy style was reassuring. I flipped another page.

Then the phone rang. The landline. An old-school device—a slimline with a squiggly cord. No caller ID. No voicemail.

Maybe it's Duguay.

Oh, come on, Cal. Don't be silly.

"Hello?"

"Hello, Cal. I saw Bruno cavorting in your backyard earlier this evening, so I assumed you'd come home."

Not Duguay. Declan. Father Mac Graith, my next-door neighbor. Colleague, friend. At least he had been until I'd begun to suspect him of colluding in Paul's spiritual conversion. The memory of this perceived slight, as well as the rudimentary details of Declan's domestic situation, had returned to me shortly after his visit to Wending Hills.

"I wondered if you'd like to join me for dinner?" There was a false brightness to his voice. "I thought you might be at a loose end."

I hesitated with an answer. Declan lived with his aged mother who, in her more lucid moments, was a damned good cook. I was tempted.

"I wouldn't want to put Mrs. Mac Graith out," I averred.

Declan coughed and then sighed.

"Mother passed away three weeks ago."

"Oh…I'm so sorry, Declan. I had no idea."

"Of course, you hadn't. You've had enough on your plate these last weeks. I didn't feel comfortable mentioning it to you while you were in hospital."

I hesitated again. Mrs. Mac Graith had been a dear lady who suffered from senile dementia. Declan gave up a career as a Church archivist to move in with his mother and care for her. I could imagine he craved diverting company, but I couldn't deal with him just yet.

"I appreciate the invite. But I don't think I'm up to it."

That was stupid. If Declan had seen Bruno, he'd most likely observed Joshua and me laughing and drinking in the sunroom the night before.

"How about later in the week?" I asked Declan. "Thursday?"

"That would be fine. By the way, I spoke with Melody today. She sends her regards. She's wondering when you might be returning to work at the center. Your students miss you."

Another jolt of guilt.

"I know. They sent me a card."

A handmade card with a brilliant caricature of me lying on a hospital bed wrapped up in bandages.

A card I'd yet to acknowledge properly.

"Well, I'll let you go, then, Cal. Have a good night."

"Goodnight, Declan."

I returned the receiver to its cradle with a dejected sigh. I'd lost all interest in Nigella, but the remainder of my cocktail called to me.

Chapter Two

I considered the next day to be my first official day back home. No Joshua, no handsome nurse practitioner. Over the years, I'd developed the habit of waking early without the aid of an alarm. It was reassuring to find myself wide awake at seven thirty, the old habit easily reestablished in familiar surroundings. The trouble was, I had no idea what to do with myself. I dithered over the preparation of coffee as I considered my choices. Gardening was a nonstarter. Shopping was also barred to me as the nearest decent shops were all within driving-only range, and the thought of calling the taxi guy for such a frivolous activity felt humiliating.

I could work, but I had no desire to do so. Angst might have been fuel for the likes of Van Gogh and Munch, but it did nothing for me. As I listened to the gurgle and plop of coffee filling the carafe, I recalled a set of sketches I'd begun just days before the accident, part of a bid for a job on a potential Broadway revival. They were awful. No concept, no focus. Just as well that someone else had surely landed the gig by now.

There was the center, of course. The Hollyford Community Center. Paul's discovery, I must admit.

Naturally gregarious and neighborly, Paul had, early on in our residence, established acquaintances with the occupants of several of the homes on our block and in the adjoining cul-de-sac. We were soon part of a clique, part of a surprisingly diverse and open-minded community. A friendship quickly developed between Paul and Father Mac Graith, and I, as Paul's "other half," had been pulled into the orbit of the Catholic priest.

"Declan's an artist, too," Paul had informed me over dinner one evening. "The community center is right next to Saint Cecelia's. He gives classes in stained glass making. Very popular. We should check it out, Cal. What do you think? Something to do together on a Saturday afternoon."

Something to do together. We could try fucking, Paul. That would be a novelty.

"Sure," I said. "Why not? It might be interesting."

And it was.

While I quickly tired of the charms of sharp glass bits and the heat and stink of the soldering iron, I got to know the director of the center, Melody Lewis, and I was soon a fly caught in her silky web.

"I'd like to extend our offerings beyond crafts and yoga," she'd said. "There are plenty of people our age—and younger folk too—who could benefit if we offered more 'serious' classes like Declan's. There's nothing wrong with old ladies making macramé angels and soccer moms playing at being hipsters, but we need to be *relevant* to all the community. I'm working on an idea for a program in conjunction with the Bingham Gallery and Hollyford Community College. Declan's class, plus life drawing, and maybe a watercolor class. What do you think?"

"Ambitious. And a great idea."

"So, would you like to come on board?"

"On board?"

"Yes. Maybe teach a class or two...?"

I smiled at Melody's wide-eyed, innocent look. She knew she'd hooked me already.

"Let me guess. Life Drawing 101 and Introduction to Watercolors?"

"I knew I could count on you."

"Melody, I think your plan is excellent. But why me?"

"You're famous."

"Hardly."

"Well, you *have* won two Tony awards. And you exhibited at the Bingham recently."

"The awards were for costume design. And I paint for pleasure... I'm not a teacher. Plus, I'm not sure if I have the time. I have other work."

The last was a lie. I hadn't had a major job in nearly a year.

"It would only be two evening classes and one Saturday."

And that was it. The beginning of my second career as a volunteer art teacher.

Two classes became four, and Saturday overflowed into Sunday.

Vague memories nudged me as I was at the point of pouring coffee into a mug decorated with cartoon images of Parisian landmarks. Something I'd missed on my sweep of couplehood memorabilia. I almost trashed it. It was ugly, yet it appealed to me on some level. Good days, maybe? Well, one reminder of happy times wasn't such a bad thing.

I limped into the mudroom which connected the kitchen to the garage. Bruno, who lay half-asleep on his bed, thumped his tail in greeting. I unlocked the French doors and carefully stepped down into the rock garden I'd created in the gap between the garage and the house. Bruno followed and curled up at my feet as I lowered myself onto a repurposed church pew.

Sipping my coffee, I looked out over the driveway to my street, Union Avenue, and to the beginning of Legion Drive at the intersection. The rambling ranch house to the left belonged to Eric Lindstrom and his wife, Jill. Bruno stood to attention and barked a greeting as Eric and his two daughters, Belinda and Susan, emerged from their front door. Susan, the youngest, waved enthusiastically and called out to Bruno. Belinda, a typical teenager, merely flipped her luxuriant blond hair and pretended she hadn't seen us. Eric followed his younger daughter's lead, then motioned them into the waiting SUV. He gave his daughters a palm-up "wait a minute" signal, then jogged across the intersection to my driveway.

"Hey!" Eric called. "You're back!"

"More or less," I replied.

"Jesus, Cal. Declan told me you'd been in an accident. I'm sorry that I—I mean we—didn't come to visit you. I was away at a convention in Arizona. Then we went to visit Jill's parents in North Carolina. Susan's been pestering me to let her visit you, but I told her you need some time alone. You know, to adjust."

He glanced over his shoulder, furtively, like a spy in an espionage film. Then he turned his face back to me. There was genuine concern there...and something else...

"I did call," Eric continued. "But your phone always went directly to voicemail. And your mailbox is full. Look, can I see you? I mean, talk? Tonight, maybe?"

"Um...sure. Okay." I was totally lost. "What time?"

"Seven? You know, Jill has her Spanish class from seven to nine thirty."

She does?

"Yeah, fine. Seven it is."

"Great." Eric flashed a brilliant smile from his strong-featured, Nordic face. "I've missed you, Cal," he added in an undertone before turning away and trotting back to his daughters.

I watched the black vehicle back out and turn down Union. Susan waved happily from her seat up front, next to her father. Behind her, Belinda leaned her face out of the open window and glared at me with clear, concentrated malevolence.

What the hell was going on?

I've missed you, Cal.

Had I missed Eric? I suppose I had—or would have, after a few days back home. Eric, Declan, and Melody were closer to being actual friends than anyone else on my list of local acquaintances. Like Joshua, most of those whom I considered friends lived in New York, and my relocation to Connecticut had, I felt, alienated many of them. Whoever coined the phrase "absence makes the heart grow fonder" was full of shit.

Stretching and raising my face to the sun, I enjoyed the heat on my skin while thinking about Eric's intensity and edginess. What could he want to discuss that was so urgent? And why that evil look from Belinda? She'd never been particularly friendly, but she'd also not been overtly hostile, as far as I could remember. Susan, on the other hand, loved to hang out with me while I worked in the front garden. I suspected her motivation was playtime with Bruno rather than lessons on planting, but she was a nice kid. It irked me that, according to Susan, her mother refused to adopt a pet for the household, claiming to have severe allergies. From what I knew of Jill, I thought it more likely she was simply being a selfish bitch.

And who's being a bitch now?

Really, who was I to judge? And I did remember gossip about the Lindstroms I'd heard from other neighbors who loved nothing more than to talk about everyone else. God knows what they said about *me* behind my back. Surprisingly, it was the late Mrs. Mac Graith, the least gossipy person I knew, who had set my mind against Eric's wife.

"Disgraceful, I call it," Elspeth Mac Graith had said to me over the fence, where I was tending to my sad-looking tomato plants. At first, I thought she was having one of her "spells" and she'd launch into a detailed description of something that had happened during the London Blitz when she was a child.

"What?" I'd asked politely, taking the bait.

"Those two," she said, tilting her head to the left. I followed the motion and looked down the dog run to the gate, then across to the Lindstrom's front lawn. "Having a row like that in *public*."

Eric and Jill were, indeed, arguing. I couldn't hear everything they were saying, but snippets such as "...the last time, Eric," "Jill, please...," and "...Okay. Fine!" came through loud and clear.

"No doubt *she's* the instigator," continued Elspeth. "No better than she should be, that one. The husband's all right. You know what his problem is, Cal?"

I shook my head.

"No balls!" pronounced Elspeth, causing me to burst out laughing.

"Laugh if you will. But I tell you, when the woman wears the pants, there's always trouble." She nodded sagely. "Always trouble."

With that, she turned abruptly and shuffled away.

Now, I wondered if she hadn't been right. Maybe that was what Eric wanted to talk about. Maybe his marriage was on the rocks, and he needed a sympathetic ear and a drink or three to cry into. I shrugged and finished off my coffee, thinking of another "maybe." Maybe listening to someone else's problems would be therapeutic.

It couldn't hurt.

Could it?

*

For the first time in a very long while, I gave thought to my attire. Not that summer weather allowed for a wide range of choices. My casual uniform of T-shirt and chinos? Oxford and chinos? Ancient, faded jeans, and a gauzy, collarless, tunic-y thing? No, no. Too sexy.

And way too young for you, buster, said a voice in my head.

Nevertheless, I put the hippy outfit aside and chose black stretch chinos and a black button-down shirt. A color cop-out, perhaps, but functional. I wasn't getting dressed for a date. I was having a drink with a likeable neighbor who was possibly having marital troubles.

All right. A likable neighbor who was possibly having marital troubles and who was also very good looking—if you're into the Norse god type. Not really my cup of tea. That's wasn't to say I hadn't occasionally fantasized when I watched Eric mowing his lawn, sweat glistening on his muscles, those little onion-skin shorts clinging to his—

Shit. I really do need to get laid.

I glanced at my watch: 6:55.

One last look in the mirror, then.

Not bad. With my straight hair falling to my shoulders, my black outfit, and my black, wolf-headed cane, I thought I'd managed an impromptu neo-goth look. It would do.

Eric arrived punctually.

No sooner had I welcomed him into the foyer and closed the door behind him, Eric stunned me by pulling me into an embrace and planting a kiss that was anything but neighborly upon my unsuspecting mouth. After a dazed moment of hesitation, I responded. Hungrily, greedily.

God, he tastes good!

Then reality hit me, and I pulled away.

"What the *hell* just happened?"

Eric laughed, reached out, and stroked my hair.

"My words, exactly, that first time. Remember?"

Remember...

"I couldn't believe it," Eric continued. "I just came over to borrow a saw blade. Next thing I know, you're on your knees giving me the best head of my life." Eric smiled, his blue eyes alight with lust.

I put more pressure on my cane as the room reeled.

"Eric...I...um."

"Cal? You all right?"

I shut my eyes, then opened them. He was still there. This was real.

"How about a drink, Eric?"

*

"Jesus," said Eric softly after downing his Teeling with the same relish as I'd once, apparently, gulped his semen. "Jesus."

Eric's one-word response to my recounting of my automobile accident, my memory loss, and my stay at Wending Hills was totally understandable. I sipped my gin and tonic, barely resisting the urge to follow Eric's example and take a large swig.

"So, you really don't remember?" Eric asked. "About...about us?"

Us? This can't be happening.

"No, Eric. Like I said, some of my memories are jumbled, some are spotty...some just aren't there at all. In time, they should all become clear. I hope."

"Jes—" Eric stopped short. "Sorry. I've got to come up with something else."

"I find that 'shit' works quite well in this sort of situation."

"How often have you been in 'this sort of situation'?"

"Never."

"Good to know."

"More whisky?"

Eric put his head in his hands and nodded. I poured a dram. When he looked up and took his tumbler, there were tears in his eyes.

A pang of tenderness hit me. Was it an echo of a past emotion, or just the intensity of the moment? Whatever it was, it was strong, compelling. I reached out and took his free hand in mine.

"Tell me, Eric. Tell me everything."

Chapter Three

ERIC

Cal, you know that story about the two doors? Or is it three? Whatever. Well, the idea is that behind one or more of the doors is something good: The Elysian fields, the pot of gold at the end of the rainbow, a new car. Behind one door, however, is a hungry lion who is waiting to do some impromptu cosmetic surgery on you with his claws before eating you alive.

The moral of the story, I guess, is that stuff happens. Sometimes, you make a choice, however mundane it may seem at the time, that leads you to the unexpected. For better or worse. Life, according to this lesson, can be like The Price is Right. Sometimes, you're better off keeping the cash rather than taking what's behind Door Number Three.

Marriage is like that. At least, it was for me.

I chose Door Number Three.

Jill was the classic "trophy wife." A blond goddess who could easily have graced the cover of Sports Illustrated or the centerfold of Playboy. The kind of wife other men drool over, the kind of wife who makes you feel like the luckiest bastard out of all your friends. Jill was beautiful. But she was so much more than that. Unfortunately, it was the "more" that I didn't take into consideration when I proposed.

We met in grad school. That alone should have been a warning to my retrograde macho vision of married life. Did I really expect a gifted student of chemistry to give up a promising career to settle into the role of a twenty-first century Jeannie?

Of course, I did.

I'd love to blame it all on my parents. I grew up in a strict, old-fashioned evangelical Lutheran household. My father was a pastor and my mother (a former Baptist) his doting helpmeet. My mother, unlike those of my contemporaries, never worked outside the realms of home and church. Mine was a happy but suffocating childhood. You'd think I would have rebelled against these outdated ideas. And I did, superficially. The usual: sex, drugs, alcohol. Truancy. But study came easily to me, and I managed to maintain honor student status and go on to win a scholarship to NYU.

A psychologist might be smiling smugly and nodding at this point.

It all comes back to your childhood.

Did I get married because I hoped to recreate some ephemeral halcyon days?

Maybe.

Probably.

Or maybe I wanted to have kids and give them something (that amorphous "something") I thought I'd missed out on when I was a child.

Very likely.

Whatever the reason, I saw a bright and happy future on the horizon with Jill as my wife. A beautiful sunrise over the mountains and, years later, a quiet and contented sunset seemed almost inevitable on the day we made our vows.

The thing is I never once thought about what Jill wanted.

Typical, you say?

Oh, yeah.

To be fair, though, Jill never communicated desires that diverged significantly from my own. And I never gave voice to my fantasy that my wife would eventually "settle down" once a child was born. Maybe I should have.

"So, what about Alvacon, then?" I asked, pouring a whisky for Jill and myself as Jill cuddled baby Belinda on her lap.

"What about it?"

Alvacon was the pharmaceutical giant for which Jill was the regional laboratory administrator.

"Well," I said, handing Jill her drink, "with the baby, and all..."

Jill snorted. "Please, Eric. Can you really see me perpetually in sweatpants and sneakers with my hair in a scrunchie? God, I'd be a frump in less than six months if I resigned. We can afford a nanny. Isn't that what we work so damned hard for?"

There it was. Switch the "we" for "I," and you can imagine how shitty I felt at that moment. Jill never missed an opportunity to remind me—always subtly, of course—

that she was the major bread winner. As a junior partner in a local accounting firm, I could hardly compete.

"Sorry, honey, I didn't mean..."

"No. Of course not. You never mean anything, Eric."

If Jill hadn't been holding our infant daughter, I might have tossed the contents of my drink in her face. I fantasized about doing it often enough. But she had the baby. Her shield, her insurance. Could I possibly have envisioned it then? That Belinda would become *her* child? Her confidant. Her coconspirator against Daddy? Did I imagine that our second child would, with bizarre logic, become *mine*? Lines were drawn that day, but it would be years before I acknowledged them.

I suppose we could have gone on in our perpetual dance of advance and retreat, thrust and parry until the girls had both left home, and then divorce quietly and civilly. Retaining familial relations with new partners with the sophisticated cordiality that so many of our recoupled friends managed.

Yeah, I guess it could have worked out that way. But, then, the elderly couple across the street in the yellow cottage died, and Cal and Paul moved in. It was the door game again. This time, however, it was Cal Restrepo who opened the door to the hungry tiger.

*

It was one of the better days: Belinda and Susan worked convivially on their respective school assignments at the dining room table, rather than holed up in their rooms with their laptops. Jill and I were busy in the kitchen preparing a meal. We both enjoyed cooking, and we found some common ground—an occasional spark of our early happiness—when we did so together.

"Calixto Restrepo," said Jill, her head in the fridge.

"Some new kind of organic lettuce?" I asked.

"No. That's his name. The Latino one with the long hair and the really nice butt."

We were discussing our new neighbors. A male couple who'd moved in the week before.

"What the hell were his parents thinking?" Jill demanded, handing me a package of endives before I could respond to the butt observation. Just as well. I could imagine my wife's reaction if I were to say something like, "You noticed that too?"

Instead, I asked, "How do you know his name?"

Jill was a mine of information about our neighborhood. It amazed be me how she managed it when she was so often away from home.

"I saw his picture in the New York Times Magazine a few weeks ago. An article about artists fleeing the city for the country. He's a costume designer and a painter."

"And the other one?"

I'd dubbed him "Lurch," owing to his height, lanky build, and somewhat dour look. Jill wasn't the only observant one.

"Paul Mangione. A biologist. Works in Stamford." Jill laughed as she chopped carrots. "He actually came over to introduce himself yesterday—you'd taken Susan with you to Stop and Shop. Can you believe it? He didn't bring cookies or a cake or anything, but I got that vibe, you know? Like he thinks because he's in suburban

Connecticut, he needs to act like June Cleaver. He's probably the bottom."

I suppressed a groan. Jill's homophobia, which she would vehemently deny, was one of the things about her that irked me the most. I had a few gay colleagues and a close gay college buddy, none of whom had taken a shine to Jill's perceived "understanding" of the "homosexual lifestyle."

"Be that as it may," I said, using one of my father's favorite phrases, "he was only trying to be friendly, Jill."

So, don't be so catty.

Fortunately, those words never left my mouth.

"True," Jill agreed. "Definitely an improvement over that old biddy, Mrs. Holm—and that nasty husband of hers."

Mr. Holm had been known to stand in his front garden and expose his privates to passersby.

"And it'll be nice to have some young people around for a change."

Jill laughed, then added, "Christ, Eric, did you ever imagine that we'd come to the point in our lives when we'd think of people in their fifties as *young*?

Jill was right. But I wondered how she'd copped their ages. Maybe it was in the article she'd read. I'd assumed they, like we, were in their mid-forties. I didn't mention this. Age was a sensitive issue with Jill. And with me, too, I must admit. There were times when Midlife Crisis seemed to loom in the shadows, smiling, holding hands with the Grim Reaper.

It wouldn't do to remark upon these insecurities to Jill, however.

"Now that you mention it, no," I said. "I guess it's because we don't *feel* our age the same way older generations did. I mean, look at our parents; they're in their sixties and seventies and still healthy and fit. Back when they were kids, people that age were in retirement homes already."

"Let's change the subject," said Jill, with a note of annoyance, as if she hadn't been the one to bring it up in the first place. I didn't point this out, of course. Keeping my mouth shut to avoid conflict had become second nature to me after twenty years of marriage.

Unfortunately, I did slip up now and then.

"Looks like they're renovating the house," I said, returning to what I thought was safe ground. "A good thing too. The Holms never so much as planted a shrub. That house was always an eyesore."

"Well," said Jill, "they're gay. And one of them is an artist. What did you expect? Maybe they can teach you something about home improvement, hon. We've been talking about fixing this place up for years, but we never seem to get around to it."

I chopped the endives. A gay stereotype followed by a dig at my manliness, nicely rounded off with one of Jill's classic we-meaning-you zingers.

"What's the point of working from home so often," Jill continued, smoothly scoring another point, "if you don't take advantage of the perks?"

I forced a smile, put the salad aside, then pulled a bottle of wine from the rack.

"You're absolutely right, dear," I replied sweetly as I applied the corkscrew with undue fervor. "You know what? Why don't we invite Calixto and Paul over for drinks one day next week? A welcome to the neighborhood kind of thing."

Jill was dumbstruck for a brief but satisfying moment.

Gotcha!

Jill disliked entertaining at home, preferring to impress her friends with cocktails and meals at overpriced restaurants.

My perceived victory was short-lived, however. Jill was gung ho about the idea.

Sometimes, you just couldn't win.

*

It was a mild evening, so we had our drinks on the deck. Jill chose Saturday, rather than a weekday, to make the gathering more relaxed—and to avoid the issue of what to do with the girls. My mother had already arranged for Belinda and Susan to stay with her over the weekend, during which time they would visit a horse farm and go bird-watching.

Jesus.

Bird-watching?

Belinda would be in a foul mood for the rest of the week, and I couldn't blame her. But she loved her grandmother, so I trusted her to behave herself. Susan, lover of all things green and/or animal would be in heaven.

A few minutes into our little cocktail party, I began to wonder if I wouldn't have been better off bird-watching.

The tension between Jill and me was like static in polyester socks that had been washed and dried without fabric softener. In contrast, Cal and Paul presented the classic united front of a happy couple. Surprisingly, though, their personalities seemed miles apart. Paul, more gregarious, gravitated toward Jill as their related fields of study and work facilitated an easy rapport. Cal seemed more of an introvert, and we stumbled over stock questions and answers, stared at our drinks, and smiled politely. I knew nothing about art, and I imagined Cal neither knew nor cared much about accounting.

I was at the point of asking God if he could be kind and end it all now, when Cal commented on the state of our large and Spartan backyard.

"You could do so much with all this space," he said, almost to himself. "The lawn is lovely, but..."

"It's boring. Yeah, I know. But I'm not much of a gardener."

"Not much of a handyman either," said Jill.

She said it with a smile, and I assumed our guests interpreted it as mild ribbing, rather than the dig that it was. They returned Jill's smile, and I went along with it, adding my own.

Then, Cal said, "And you, Jill? Are you handy with a hammer or a spade?"

Butter, as the saying goes, wouldn't have melted in Cal's mouth. His black eyes, however, hinted at provocation.

Thank you, Cal.

Jill, either oblivious to Cal's subtle snark or sensing she'd met her match, answered truthfully. "No. I don't have the patience or the skill. And I can't stand creepy-crawly things."

"Well, Eric," said Paul, "if you ever need a hand with a job, I'd be happy to help you out."

Cal sniggered as he sipped his cocktail, and Jill raised an eyebrow. Paul made a face and play-punched Cal's shoulder.

I was clueless. "Did I miss something?"

"Nothing, honey," said Jill, looking at me with a surprising glint of affection in her eyes. "I'll explain it later."

"Seriously," said Paul. "We've got spare tools. You can come over and grab whatever—"

Cal interrupted with a snort of amusement, and I finally caught on.

"Are you quite finished?" Paul asked of Cal.

"Yes, dear," Cal answered with mock contrition. "Just don't mention drills. Or screws."

Cal's sophomoric silliness lightened the atmosphere and my mood. It also made me look at Cal for the first time. I mean, *really* look. His eyes were incredibly dark. So dark that only in a certain light could you tell they were brown, not the same black lacquer shade of his hair, which he wore in a Japanese-style topknot. It was fashionable, I supposed, but it also suited him. It set off the strong bone structure of his face perfectly. I imagined him as a warrior, naked except for an animal skin loincloth, the golden-brown skin of his compact, tightly muscled body glistening with sweat. My mind was aware that my fantasy was tinged with racism, but my cock didn't seem to care. I crossed my legs to hide my erection, though a sly half-smile from Cal told me the effort was wasted. Of course, I'd wanted him to see it, hadn't I?

I reigned in my wild thoughts, but my hand shook a little as I raised my tumbler to my lips and took a gulp. I had always fantasized about other men, but I'd never acted on those fantasies. And I had certainly never flashed a boner to a neighbor in my own backyard.

"I appreciate the offer, Paul." I looked away from Cal, back to his partner. "Of help with the renovation project," I clarified, producing smiles all around. I turned to Jill. "I guess I'm officially committed, darling."

Jill laughed and raised her martini. "Here's to commitment!"

The toast went around, and Jill leaned over and kissed me. She seemed happy. But I knew it was happiness at finally having cornered me into the reno— not happiness in our marriage. I looked across at Paul and Cal, their hands entwined on the tabletop, and a wave of jealousy swept over me.

We used to be like that.

Then it struck me that their hands were not actually entwined; Cal had reached out and covered Paul's with his own. The gesture was a sign, a symbol—just as Jill's kiss had been. What did it mean? Had Jill observed the brief exchange between Cal and me? Was the kiss a warning? Likewise, was Cal subtly telling me that despite his complicit smile, he was happily monogamous? My social skills ranked right up there with my handyman credentials, so maybe I was totally wrong. But there was a current of *something* that even I could sense.

*

It would be a while before I saw much of Cal again. Paul and I were destined to become weekend buddies as we began our home improvement projects, and Jill surprised me by falling into an easy friendship with Paul. Cal spent a good deal of his weekend hours teaching at the community center, so a four-way relationship never developed, a good thing as far as Jill was concerned.

"I mean, he's so *typical*," said Jill as we slowed to a jog at the intersection. We shared a love of running. Sometimes, I wondered if it was what had kept us together for so long.

"Typical of what?"

We were discussing our new neighbors during the cruise interval of our morning tempo run. More than a month had passed since the cocktail party.

"I should say stereotypical," Jill amended. "The *artiste*. The bitchy queen. I don't understand what Paul sees in him."

He's handsome. He's funny. And I bet he's hot as hell in the sack.

"Maybe that's just Cal's persona," I said aloud. "The *at home* Cal could be someone entirely different."

"Jung's theories aside," said Jill, tucking a stray lock of blond hair into her loose bun. "I just think Paul's really nice and down to earth. He deserves better."

She'd made her pronouncement. The topic was closed.

And I had to admit I could see her point. Cal and Paul were an oddly matched couple. But wasn't that the type of couple whose relationship usually succeeded? Opposites did attract?

As I ran—perfectly in sync with my wife—I thought no one could be more opposite of Jill than Calixto Restrepo. And there was no denying I felt a strong attraction to him.

That man will be your undoing.

It was my father's voice I heard in my head, resonant and in full ministerial mode.

Maybe, Dad. But I'm forty-five years old. I think I'm overdue for an undoing.

I spent the rest of the day working from my home office. When I say "working," I mean that I stared at spreadsheets, drank coffee, shuffled files, and accomplished nothing. The work I had pending could have been completed within thirty minutes with a concentrated effort but remained incomplete when the girls returned home from school.

Belinda breezed in and out, staying just long enough to say hello, exchange her school uniform for street clothes, and say goodbye. It was mani-pedi day. I felt a pang of loss as I watched her get into her car and drive away. Before long, she'd be in college. Seventeen years gone in a flash. I realized I hardly knew my eldest daughter, and I might have lost the chance of ever doing so. I was staring forlornly out the window with coffee mug in hand when Susan knocked politely on the doorframe.

"Dad?"

"What's up, doc?" I spun my chair around to greet Susan with a smile of relief and happiness. At least I hadn't messed up twice. I hadn't failed Susan as I'd failed her sister and her mother.

"Cal's planting stuff in his front garden. Do you think he'd mind if I went over to see what it is?"

Susan had inherited my mother's green thumb, but so far, her efforts had been limited to houseplants.

"If you ask politely, I'm sure he won't mind."

I pretended I hadn't observed her over there previously, playing with Cal's dog.

"And I bet he's got that ugly mutt with him, right?" I asked.

Susan had given up on the can-we-please-get-a-dog question long ago, but I knew she was still secretly pining. Frequent visits to my parents and their three Labradors didn't help. I smiled at the memory of my mother pointing out sweetly to Jill that there were pills available to counteract her dog allergy. "You must know that, dear," she'd said. "You work for a pharmaceutical company, after all." Good one, Mom.

"His name is Bruno, Dad. And he's not ugly. He's unique."

"If you say so, sweetheart. Tell Cal I said hi."

Susan swept a glance over the mess on my desk, my rumpled flannel shirt, and my bare feet.

"You really need to get out, Dad. Why don't you come with me?"

Why not?

"Okay." I got up and smoothed my shirt, looked around for my sneakers.

"You're not going out like *that*, are you?"

Having just turned eleven, Susan was at that age when everything her parents did was potentially embarrassing.

"What do you suggest? A top hat and tails?

"Hilarious, Dad. Something clean will do."

"Yes, Ma'am!" I gave a sharp salute, to which Susan responded with a sigh and a shake of her Shirley Temple curls.

"Parents today," she lamented. "What are we going to do with them?"

"Give me ten minutes, okay? I'll meet you there."

"Cool."

Susan gave me a tight hug.

"Make that fifteen minutes, Dad," she said, standing back and wrinkling her nose. "You need a shower."

"Get out, monkeyface. See you in fifteen."

Fourteen minutes later, squeaky clean and clad in a bulky gray cable-knit sweater and faded 501's, I made my way across the street.

Susan sat cross-legged with Bruno on her lap, and Cal was on his knees digging in the earth. I tried not to stare at Cal's upturned buttocks, but I could not help but notice he wore no underwear. His smooth, deeply cleft brown ass was clearly visible above the low-slung waistband of his gray sweats.

"I think I've left planting them too late," he said dejectedly, sitting back on his haunches. "Unless we have a late first frost this year."

"What are they?" I asked.

"Tulips. Purple ones," said Cal.

"They're called queen of the night," added Susan, picking up a package and showing me the picture."

"Beautiful." I looked from the package to Cal. I thought the same could be said of Cal's glossy hair. A few strands of silver glinted in the sunlight as he brushed it back with his fingers. I wondered what it would be like to touch it, to stroke it. Cal smiled, and I could swear he knew what I was thinking.

"We shall see," said Cal. "You're supposed to plant them when the earth is cool, but well before the first frost."

"How do you know when the earth is cool?" asked Susan.

Cal shrugged. "No idea. The more I read about planting bulbs, the more confused I get. But, apparently, October is the latest you should plant in this area. I think. If they don't bloom, I'll go with plan B."

"What's plan B?"

"Grass."

I laughed. "I believe you said grass is boring."

"*You* said grass is boring. I just don't relish the idea of mowing it."

"You don't have to do it yourself," chimed in Susan with the tone of a teacher instructing a less-than-bright pupil. "We get a Mexican guy to do ours."

Oh, for fuck's sake!

I could just hear Jill or Belinda saying the same thing to a friend while she had her nails buffed by a Korean "girl."

I gave Cal an apologetic look and felt like a worm.

"Susan, honey," I said as gently as I could, "we've had this discussion before. You don't identify people by their color or their country of origin. Or their race. It's very rude."

"I'm sorry, Daddy. But he *is* Mexican. I mean—"

Susan stopped suddenly, and she turned her gaze to Cal. The look of stunned realization on her face would have been comical under different circumstances.

"Oh..." Susan put her hand to her mouth and blushed with embarrassment. "I'm sorry, Cal. I didn't mean anything bad about Tomas—that's the lawn-mowing guy—or, um, Latino people... I'm sorry."

Cal surprised me by smiling. He went over to Susan, sat down next to her, and put his hand on top of hers where it lay on Bruno's flank.

"I'm sure you didn't, Susan. But your dad's right. Part of growing up is learning not to offend people, even unintentionally. I mean, do you think that when I talk about you to my friends, I call you the 'white girl' who lives across the street?"

Susan shook her lowered head.

"Of course not," continued Cal. "I call you the 'little brat.'"

Susan's head snapped up at this, and Cal laughed.

"You see?"

Susan grinned. "I get it, Cal. And I think you're really cool."

"Thanks."

"And what about me?" I asked my daughter.

"Oh, yeah. You're cool, too, Daddy."

"Good save, Monkeyface."

Bruno stirred, climbed off Susan, and wiggled.

"I think Mr. Bruno wants to take a walk," said Cal. "He's bored with tulips and lessons on social interaction."

"Can I walk him, Cal? Please?"

"Susan," I began, "I don't think—"

"Don't worry, Eric," Cal said. "It's okay. Bruno's taken a shine to Susan, and he's as gentle as a lamb." He turned to Susan. "His lead and some plastic bags are just inside the mudroom." Cal pointed to the open French doors. "On the left side."

"Thanks, Cal!"

Susan took off in search of Bruno's leash, and the dog trotted expectantly behind her. I sat down next to Cal.

"I should thank you too. You handled that well. Susan's got her head screwed on right, I think. She just picks up stuff from her moth—um—from kids at school, I guess."

Cal nodded. "You seem to be doing a good job. She's a nice kid."

"Thanks. Did you ever—"

I stopped short, unsure if the question I had in my head was appropriate.

"Ever what?"

"Nothing. Forget it."

Susan returned, Bruno well in hand.

"Don't go too far, honey," I admonished.

"To the river and back?"

The river. That made me smile. It was nothing more than a narrow, picturesque stream dividing a street, but Susan was still young enough to imagine it as a grand place of adventure.

"Okay. But no farther. You have your phone?"

"Yes, Dad."

Susan turned to Cal. "Thanks again, Cal. I'll take good care of him; I promise."

And off they went.

Cal stood and brushed soil from his pants.

"How about a drink while we await Susan's return from the wilderness?"

"Sounds perfect."

"Gin and tonic okay?"

"Sure."

Cal returned shortly with the drinks on a tray and two folding chairs. I relieved him of the chairs and opened them, facing them in the direction in which Susan and Bruno had set out.

"Thanks," I said as I sat and accepted a highball glass from Cal. "Cheers."

"Cheers."

We sipped our drinks in silence for a few moments, appreciating the cool autumn breeze and the last of the waning sunshine.

Eventually, Cal turned to me and asked: "So, what was the 'ever'?"

"Hum?"

"You asked me, 'Did you ever...' I'm curious to know *what*."

I shifted in my canvas chair, uncomfortable with the prodding, yet accepting Cal's interest and my responsibility for half broaching the question that had been on my mind.

"I'm not sure how to ask this," I began, "or even if I should. But, well, you seemed so easy with Susan. I mean, you've got a knack with kids, I think. Um…did you ever think about having children… No, that's not right…you might have children already… I mean… Jesus, I feel like Susan, talking about Mexicans mowing lawns!"

"Please," Cal said. "You shouldn't try to be politically correct. I never do. It's too complicated." He took a drink. "Although you do look awfully cute when you blush."

I *felt* the blush this time, seeping up from my neck to my cheeks and to the roots of my crew-cut blond hair.

Cal laughed. "I'm a tease, Eric. Don't take me seriously."

I imagined a glint in Cal's dark eyes. "A tease about everything?"

"Oh, no."

The huskiness in his voice was undeniable. My pulse quickened, and my prick twitched uncomfortably in the confines of my jeans. But after a few moments of silence and a couple of pulls on our drinks, Cal threw water on the fire of my lustful thoughts by returning to my previous question.

"Yes," he said softly. "I have thought about having children. Paul and I talked about it a lot when we first met. But it never got past talk. Now…"

Cal shrugged. "Well, we're both easing into our fifties. I know people start families at our age nowadays…but…I just feel like I'm past it. And I think Paul feels the same. We don't talk about it anymore. We're set in our ways…used to being just us."

I heard sadness in Cal's words but didn't feel I knew him well enough to pursue the subject, though I did appreciate the irony when comparing our situations. I loved my daughters—and I still loved Jill, despite our differences—but there was always a nagging regret somewhere inside me; a little voice that asked me if I'd made the right choice in marrying and having children. Cal regretted not having had them and felt it was too late for him to do so now.

Cal saved me from trying to come up with a smooth segue to another topic. "Anyway, I have students now—you know I've started teaching classes at the community center—and in some ways, being a teacher is like being a parent. Maybe this was my destiny."

"You believe in predestination?"

Cal considered the question for a moment, slipping into a slouch and swirling the contents of his glass.

"I'm not sure I *believe* in anything, Eric. I acknowledge possibilities."

I did not respond verbally, but looked a question at Cal, holding his gaze, and I had the answer in the glimmer glancing off the dark surfaces of his eyes.

I was one of those possibilities.

Chapter Four

CAL

I recalled that day in October quite clearly. I remembered planting the bulbs. I remembered Susan and her polite questions about gardening. I remembered Eric's arrival on the scene, even the color and texture of the sweater he wore. I remembered Susan's innocent racial faux pas and her taking Bruno for a walk to the "river." I even remembered the frisson of attraction between Eric and me. I did not, however, recall feeling such an overwhelming sexual desire for my neighbor that I would, just a few weeks later, literally throw myself at his feet.

It had happened before though. Once. It was during the first year of my relationship with Paul, with a very attractive guy from the costume shop I was working with for a period piece at a theater in Los Angeles. I considered it a lay. He had other ideas. It was ugly but blessedly brief, and it taught me a valuable lesson in self-control.

But...

If it happened once, I thought to myself as Eric described our first sexual encounter and subsequent affair, wasn't it quite likely it might have happened again?

Had I been the Whore of Babylon? The neighborhood *puta*? I certainly had the libido to support the character, yet I just couldn't see myself in the role. But with Eric, there was something deeper, a connection I'd felt from our first meeting.

It's true. It's really true.

I looked at Eric, his six-two, broad shouldered frame folded into the leather sling chair by the fireplace, and I believed it was true. I knew it was true. Any emotional bond aside, I couldn't deny my sexual attraction to Eric. And Paul and I hadn't made love for many months before his departure. Oh, yes, I believed everything Eric told me. It hit me like a truck—the suppressed memories, the blank months corresponding with the affair. It all made devastatingly perfect sense.

"I see" was my succinct response to Eric's outpouring.

Eric looked down at the glossy wood floor and wrung his hands, reminding me of a bad actor in a telenovela.

"I don't know what else to say, Cal. If you don't remember, what can I do?" Eric stopped wringing his hands and swiped one over his face in a gesture of frustration. "This is crazy."

"Trust me, I know."

"Sorry. I mean...I...I'm sorry."

What possessed me to do what I did next? Remembered feelings of affection for Eric that had somehow welled up during his discourse? Loneliness? A stray stab of vindictiveness toward Paul? Horniness? Probably all of these rolled into one. A voice in my head—

which spoke with Joshua's Received Pronunciation—told me I was being a fool. But I went to Eric, nonetheless. I went to him and opened my arms to him. I held him. We kissed. Then, with the utmost care and gentleness, Eric picked me up and carried me to bed.

*

He didn't stay very long afterward. Of course, he didn't; he had his family waiting for him. I lay in the sea of rumpled sheets in a state of bittersweet languor. Eric was a good lover. No, he was an *excellent* lover. His kisses, his strokes, his caresses; his whispers and urgent hisses had combined to take me to a point at which I no longer felt any pain in my body. I felt nothing but the thrum and heat of desire, the heart-thumping ache to have him inside me.

Please, I had said, over and over. *Please...*

When was the last time I had begged for it? Surrendered completely and shamelessly to physical need. Had I ever? Of course, it wasn't just physical need. It was emotional, mental, spiritual—every want, every desire, every unfulfilled dream brought into laser-sharp focus and channeled through carnality to be expiated in the final hot blasts of ejaculation.

You really are full of shit, Calixto! It was a hot fuck, and you needed it badly. It wasn't a tantric transcendental experience. It's over, he's gone, and you're alone again.

I didn't need the missing memories to know this was how it must have always been with Eric. I was the "other man," after all. However, my lack of recall of past intimacies with Eric disturbed me. Even if I could not remember the actual days, times, and specific events, surely some *sense* memory would have been sparked by Eric's touch, his scent, the way he felt inside me. But there was nothing. It was as if it had been our first time. Was this a precursor of things to come? Would I meet old friends, possess clear memories of them, yet lack an emotional connection—an emotional memory?

I pushed these ruminations aside and concentrated on the impracticality, never mind the immorality, of my relationship with Eric.

It must end, I told myself as I slogged to the bathroom for a much-needed shower. *Before it becomes more complicated.*

*

Duguay had checked my vitals, and I was preparing coffee while he sat in the breakfast nook making notes on his laptop. There was a companionable silence as we went about our duties, punctuated now and then by the click of Duguay's keyboard or the gurgle of the coffee machine.

The events of the previous day seemed distant and bizarre when contemplated in the air of quiet confidence and good cheer which Duguay brought with him. His presence enabled me to compartmentalize the anxiety I harbored over my relationship with Eric and concentrate on positive thoughts. The song "Happy Talk" from the musical *South Pacific* popped into my head, and I snorted a laugh as I selected tableware.

Duguay looked up from his laptop, his eyebrows raised quizzically over the frames of his reading glasses.

"Would you like to share?" he asked. "Or is it something too personal?"

"Yes," I said. Then, "No."

Duguay's eyebrows remained up.

"I was having a Rodgers and Hammerstein moment," I confessed. I arranged the coffee service on the tray, intending to deliver it myself; but Duguay was at my side before I could attempt it.

"Allow me," he said, reaching for the tray. He looked at me and smiled, his eyes sparkling with humor and a sort of fey mischief. Or maybe it was just a trick of his eyeglass lenses. "What song was it? 'Some Enchanted Evening'?"

I returned the smile, imagining Duguay in the role of the stranger across a crowded room, and a sudden flutter passed through my chest. *Mariposas en el corazon* as my father would have said. Butterflies in the heart.

"No," I replied. 'Happy Talk.'"

Duguay shocked me by bursting into song, delivering the refrain along with the accompanying hand gestures.

When I'd stopped laughing, I said: "You have a great voice."

Duguay shrugged. "Thanks. My parents were both musical theater actors before they retired and opened their garden center business. When I was a kid, I wanted to be a singer and dancer. But I knew I didn't have what it took to succeed."

"What?" I asked, disbelieving. "Good looks and talent?"

"I had *really* bad acne, wore glasses, and was painfully shy. Plus, I couldn't dance my way out of a paper bag. The first finally disappeared when I was in my early twenties, the second could have been corrected with contact lenses, but the third was the deal-breaker."

I smiled at Duguay's sincerity.

"And you?" Duguay asked.

"I had flawless skin, was one of the 'popular' kids, and could do a mean salsa and tango."

"Don't forget the sarcastic wit. I meant—what did you want to be when you grew up?"

I followed Duguay to the breakfast nook and poured out our coffee.

"I think I always wanted to be an artist of some kind," I said, properly answering Duguay's query. "I painted and toyed with sculpture through grammar school and high school. I started college intent on becoming a fashion designer but switched to costume design after my first year. I thought the fashion industry would be too creatively limiting. I fantasized about being the next Saint Laurent, but the reality was I'd probably have spent my career churning out boring clothing anonymously for some big label or retailer."

"You wanted to be famous?"

"No. Not really. What I wanted was to love what I did. When I moved to costume design, I knew I'd found my niche. How did you discover medicine?"

"It wasn't a vocation, but the interest was always there, in the background. I was fascinated with biology and science. I excelled at it. My original plan was to be a researcher, not a clinician, but after my first stint of volunteer work at a hospital, I realized I enjoyed working with people and had a good rapport with patients. It just...happened, I guess."

"And here you are."

"And here I am."

We sipped our coffee in silence, looking out at the garden—and occasionally at each other.

"Shouldn't we get to work?" I asked eventually, breaking the spell of contentment mixed with subdued, amorphous anticipation.

"Do you really want to?" Duguay replied, surprising me.

"No."

Duguay smiled and heaved a sigh. "However, when needs must..."

Quickly resuming his professional demeanor, Duguay outlined my exercise plan.

"Do you own a treadmill?" he asked.

"No."

"Good. There's no better encouragement to recovery than fresh air and sunshine. And your neighborhood looks like it has the perfect balance of straight paths and gentle inclines. A heart monitor and a stopwatch are all the equipment we need."

"Can Bruno tag along?"

Duguay considered my request. I wondered if he realized I was testing him.

"If he lets me hold his lead, sure. Until you're a bit stronger and less reliant on the cane, you really should consider hiring a dog walker. Bruno's adorable, by the way. I'd like to have a dog myself, but my schedule doesn't allow me enough time to be a good animal parent."

Passed with flying colors.

I wasn't ready to think about *why* it mattered to me whether Duguay liked Bruno—or dogs in general. Considering Paul's desertion and Eric's bombshell about our clandestine affair, I knew I was on shaky ground where relationships were concerned. But I admit I felt a click of sympathy with Duguay.

We set out on our walk and had passed beyond Susan's river before we spoke, Duguay initiating the conversation.

"Have you given any thought to when you'll begin driving again? You're physically capable."

The question came out of nowhere, and I was served with a sharp reminder of who Duguay was and who had arranged for his services. Potential friendship aside, Duguay had a job to do. I looked down at the cane under my hand and thought about how relatively easily I'd managed being back home, tackling day-to-day activities. I really didn't need a nurse. Then, the other shoe dropped. I recalled one of the many acronyms following Duguay's name on his laminated credentials: CP. Clinical psychologist.

"You're Malhotra's henchman," I said, casting a sidelong glance at Duguay. "I should have realized. All this crap about physical therapy is just an excuse for monitoring what's going on in my head—to make 100 percent sure I'm safe outside the looney bin, right?"

Duguay stopped walking. I followed suit. Bruno sat down with a huff.

"Look, Cal," Duguay said with a touch of frost in his voice. "Dr. Malhotra is not a villain from a James Bond flick, and I am not a *henchman*. I'm here to monitor your recovery—both physical and emotional—and make reports and recommendations to your physician. I believe I made that clear at our first meeting."

You might have, but I was paying more attention to the shape of your mouth than to the words coming out of it.

"Sorry," I mumbled. "That question hit me like a left hook."

"I know. Catching someone off guard on a sensitive subject is a method used to obtain honest answers. Sometimes it works, sometimes it just pisses people off. In your case, I think I'm probably better off using charm."

I turned my gaze from the pavement to Duguay, knowing he was smiling now, the edge gone from his voice.

"But that has its dangers, too," he added.

"Such as...?"

"I think you know, Cal," said Duguay.

"Um...fraternizing and whatnot?"

Duguay laughed his throaty laugh.

"Fraternization is often par for the course," he said. "It's the whatnot that could be a problem."

"You see a potential for whatnot?" I asked.

Duguay didn't answer my question. Well, not verbally. But I thought by the look in his eyes that the answer was "yes."

"Let's get back on track," said Duguay. Maybe I only imagined a tinge of regret in his voice.

"By all means," I agreed as we resumed our walk.

"You need to think about driving again, Cal. I understand the emotional roadblocks—pardon the expression—but it's essential that you surmount them. Otherwise, those emotional blocks could cripple you permanently. If you were living in New York, it would be a secondary, even tertiary concern. But here..." Duguay waved a hand to encompass my suburban enclave. "Without a car, you could become a recluse. Physical isolation could lead to mental isolation. You need to avoid that path. Tempting as it may seem now."

"I know."

And I did. I'd already experienced the insidious desire to hibernate, to close myself off. I thought of how I'd brushed off Declan's invitation, ignored the well-wishes of my students and Melody.

We walked a little bit more in silence, approaching Main Street and the green that bisected it. There were quaint wrought iron benches there, facing a large gazebo which served as a bandstand on festive occasions. At Duguay's suggestion, we sat on one of the benches.

"Giving me a rest already?"

"Only your legs. This seems like a nice place to relax and talk."

I let out a disgruntled sigh.

"Don't worry, Cal. This isn't a 'session.' But I need to ask you a few things. Standard questions. I would have done so earlier this morning, but Rogers and Hammerstein intervened."

"Okay, shoot."

Duguay pulled a small notebook and a mechanical pencil from his jacket and began.

"Have you experienced any unusually bizarre or disturbing dreams?"

"No. And no thoughts of suicide or periods of sudden, debilitating sadness."

"Please, Cal. Let me pose the questions before you supply answers."

"Sorry."

"All right, then," said Duguay, scribbling something in shorthand. "Any thoughts of suicide or periods of sudden, debilitating sadness?"

"You're a real card, you know that, Duguay?"

"When you're ready to be serious, then so shall I."

"Shall you, indeed?" I asked archly. Duguay opened his mouth to respond, but I put up a peremptory hand. "If you answer 'yes, I shall,' we're going to sound like Chip and Dale."

"Who?"

"The chipmunks."

Duguay looked bewildered. "I have no idea what you're talking about, Cal."

"Forget it. Ask your questions. I'll be serious."

"Thank you." He opened the notebook once more. "Have you experienced any dizziness or nausea?"

"No."

"Euphoria?"

Does a toe-curling orgasm count?

"No."

"Confusion?"

I shook my head.

"Very good," said Duguay. "I can see that those meds you haven't been taking are doing the trick." He twitched a smile at my abashed look. "It's all right. Most of them are palliatives and pain relievers. If you really feel you don't need them..." Duguay shrugged and wrote more shorthand. "As to the propranolol—the one for confusion—well, I'm a psychologist, not a psychiatrist. I've never been too keen on pushing pills."

Duguay looked at me closely, trying to communicate something with it. I remembered his words earlier that day regarding my refusal to take my meds: *"I didn't hear that."* He was intimating I should do the same about his last statements. I nodded.

"So, then, Mr. Restrepo," Duguay continued. "Have you been taking all of your medications as indicated?"

"Yes, Nurse Practitioner Duguay."

"Excellent. Now, have you seen any improvement in your memory? Any setbacks?"

"Well..."

How could I explain to Duguay about my experience with Eric, my uneasiness with my lack of recall, without revealing our relationship? And why should it matter? I didn't have to name Eric. But I felt uncomfortable exposing my affair to Duguay. I liked him, and I wanted him to like me. Admitting I'd cheated on my partner didn't seem like a great way to make that happen.

Think of something else.

"I spent time with my old friend Joshua the other day," I said. "He came to visit when I returned home from Wending Hills. While we were talking, I felt lost at times—not remembering people clearly, recalling the name but not the face—that sort of thing. But since then, a lot has come back to me. I feel more focused, if that makes any sense."

Duguay nodded. "Being in a familiar, comfortable environment should have that effect."

"Then why was Dr. Malhotra so reluctant to send me home?"

Duguay took his time responding, and I wondered why. Was he deciding between the truth and something more palatable? I hadn't gotten a straight answer from any doctor or nurse since my accident, but I had higher hopes for Duguay.

He shifted his body toward me, put a hand on my shoulder, and said, "Because you had no one to go home to."

Okay. So maybe I didn't want a straight answer as much as I thought I did.

"Oh..."

"Cal," continued Duguay, removing his hand. "I don't know any of the details of your domestic life, except what you shared with me the other day in your garden. Dr. Malhotra only informed me that you lived alone. She felt that put you at risk. Initially, she asked a friend of yours—a Mr. Summerly, I believe—if he could stay with you for a few weeks. But he declined."

"What?"

Duguay smiled. "Strictly off the record, according to Dr. Malhotra, Mr. Summerly informed her that you're a stubborn bastard and would never accept his offer. He said you would only submit to assistance under duress."

"Enter Nurse Practitioner Duguay."

"At your service."

"Well," I said, "you're not duress-ing me—if that's a word. In fact, you're one of the least duress-ing people I've ever met."

"It isn't and thank you."

I've never managed a poker face, and I suppose Duguay was professionally disposed to recognize signs of unease or prevarication. He studied me for a few moments.

"Anything else?" he asked. "Any other memories... recollections of the more recent events that have eluded you so far?"

"Um...there was something else," I replied, my conscience easing as I committed to the revelation. I took a deep breath, thought of backpedaling, and then settled upon honesty.

"I cheated on Paul."

There, it's done.

"What triggered the memory?"

No judgement in Duguay's tone, only professional interest.

"Um...well, it wasn't a memory—not exactly."

"Explain."

Flashback to my fifth year in parochial school: I was sitting in an uncomfortable metal chair waiting for the principle to pronounce some heinous corporal punishment in recompense for my sin of shoving snow into the nose of the recess monitor, Mrs. Gonzales. Rather than rant against the unconscionable behavior of a willful, sinful child or whack my knuckles with a ruler, Sister Anne had leaned forward across her desk and, with the most earnest expression upon her face, said: "Explain."

Duguay could not have been less like Sister Anne in appearance, but the searching, curious look in his eyes was unnerving in its similarity to that of the nun.

"Well..." I brushed my hands over my knees and looked away. I might just as well have been eleven years old again.

"Yes?"

"All right. It's like this. The person with whom I— No, that sounds ridiculous. The guy I fucked told me all about it."

"Shit."

"Yup."

Silence drew out between us.

"He didn't know about my memory loss," I added, not sure that it mattered.

"You must tell him, Cal."

"I did."

"And?"

"We fucked again."

It was Duguay's turn to look away. When he looked back, his expression was inscrutable, the professional mask firmly in place.

"And you have clear memories of this... entanglement?"

Entanglement? Leave it to a pro to come up with the best description.

"That's the thing, Marc," I said, unconsciously using Duguay's given name for the first time. "I don't, really. I mean, I remember *him*. I remember the attraction. But doing the deed? No. And it felt strange afterward...this last time. It was as if it was the *first* time. I really don't know how else to explain it."

Duguay regarded me with his head cocked to one side, his eyelids lowered.

"So, you think this is it? The reason for your memory blackout...the missing pieces?"

"It must be," I said softly. "Malhotra is convinced that my memory lapse is the result of emotional trauma...some repressed memory. I'd say this fits the bill, wouldn't you?"

Rather than answer, Duguay posed a question.

"Did you ever discuss this with Paul?"

Hello!

"Are you crazy?" I demanded. "What good would that have done? Paul left me to follow a religious calling. I don't see how admitting to an affair at that point would have made any difference."

Something akin to a sad smile flitted across the lower half of Duguay's face.

"Assuming, of course," said Duguay, "that Paul didn't know."

It might sound naïve—stupid, really—but I never considered the possibility. Suddenly, Malhotra's words hit me with newfound gravitas: *"There are those who believe that everything that happens to us is, in some way, our own fault."*

Then Paul's words:

"It's not you, Cal. It's me."

Which was the truth? Or was there a perfect storm of a gray area I had yet to remember, understand, or consider?

I lowered my head and brought my palms up to meet my face.

"I'm a mess, Duguay," I muttered.

Duguay's hand rested on my shoulder once more.

"If you told me you felt fine and that everything was hunky-dory, then I'd be worried."

Hunky-dory?

"I guess you have a point," I said, looking up. "I have to stop feeling sorry for myself. I think the first thing I need to do is go back to work."

Duguay made a small moue with his lips and simultaneously raised his eyebrows. I recognized it as his "considering" look.

"It would certainly help to sharpen your concentration," he allowed. "And engaging in a routine activity in another familiar environment should encourage memory recuperation."

"But?" I asked. The "but" had been loud and clear in Duguay's response.

"You need to be careful not to allow the activity to become a crutch."

"How so?"

"Using work as a way to avoid taking emotional stock and dealing with the trauma you've experienced since your partner's departure and his subsequent death."

"I thought I'd been there and done that at Wending Hills," I replied.

"Nothing's ever really *over*, Cal. You can't just brush the feelings away like dust from your hands and say, 'that's that, all gone.' Everything we experience becomes part of who we are. Trying to deny or avoid that truth is where the real trouble lies. I think you proved this to yourself today."

I favored Duguay with my best side-eye.

"I liked you better when you were just a physical therapist."

"All right, then," said Duguay, standing and stretching. "Let's get physical."

*

I was tired after my hour-long trek around the neighborhood. Duguay pushed just enough to allow me to obtain that feeling of exhilaration that accompanies a good workout without crossing my pain threshold, which wasn't nearly as high as I thought it was. I winced as I rotated my shoulder under the warm spray of the shower. I would have loved to have taken a long soak in the tub. And it was part of Duguay's brief to assist me with such activities. But by an unspoken agreement we avoided this physical intimacy. Instead, he waited outside until I was safely washed, dried, and clothed. It spoke to the relationship developing between us that we both apparently considered Duguay seeing me naked as an intimacy rather than a professional duty. At least, I wanted to think so.

Duguay left me with a hug rather than a handshake, and I savored the quick embrace, taking in the scent of him—warm, exotic, and almost frustratingly delicate. He wore scent the way it was meant to be worn, applied sparingly so as only to be detected at close contact or on a chance waft of air.

"Until Monday, then," said Duguay with a final pat on my shoulder.

God, I want to kiss you. I want to taste your mouth and feel the wild brown curls of your hair between my fingers. I want—

"Until Monday."

*

Declan's house was a late-forties Cape, an excrescence of interior doors and windows too small and too high to provide any decent light. Larger than my cottage yet smaller than Eric's rambling sixties ranch, it was emblematic of the cheap and quickly built residences designed for the returning GI's of World War Two.

With a front garden perpetually gray, rocky, brown, and overgrown—an intentional but unfortunate design choice on Declan's part—I could never pass the property without the Munsters' theme song popping into my head. I found myself humming the first few bars as I depressed the ringer of the doorbell and heard the Westminster chime.

Declan answered the door clad in his usual off-duty uniform of old jeans, T-shirt, and sandals. He wasn't an unattractive man, was still in good shape with an open, welcoming face (good qualities for a man of the cloth, I suppose). But his unkempt, bushy eyebrows and prematurely gray hair ruined the overall effect. Maybe that was because he reminded me of my third-grade teacher—a nun with the same eyebrows and a mole on her nose, who stuffed dirty Kleenex under the sleeve of her habit. Another one of those crystal-clear memories of unpleasant people, places, and things.

"Hello, Cal."

In the gloom of the boxy foyer, I endured a rather close pastoral embrace, finding Declan's artificial smell of Ivory soap and fabric softener almost repulsive compared to Duguay's botanical concoction.

"Thanks for the invite, Declan," I said as he released me. "I should have given you a call to let you know when I was coming back. It's just that everything's been a jumble, and—"

"Say no more, Cal. I understand completely. With Mother's passing, I'm afraid I've found myself in much the same situation." He presented me with one of his stiff-upper-lip, soldier-on smiles. "Though, really," he continued, "Mother's death was hardly a surprise—and a relief in many ways. The Lord blessed her with a swift and timely deliverance."

And you were delivered as well, weren't you?

"Come on in," said Declan, opening the door to the living room.

The room was empty, save for a well-worn sofa and two chairs. All of Elspeth's knickknacks, doilies, antimacassars, and porcelain statuary were gone.

Cardboard boxes sat in a neat line before the empty fireplace.

"You're leaving," I said, surprised at the sadness I felt at this realization.

Declan nodded. "I only had this place because of Mother's condition, you know. Now she's gone, I've got to move on as well."

"Will you be going back to Rome?"

A pinched, negative look passed over Declan's face. "No. That bridge is burned. Father Regenmacher is retiring." Declan referred to the rector of Saint Cecelia's, the beachside church adjacent to the community center. "I'll be replacing him."

"An easy transition, at least," I said. Declan had served as backup (or whatever the correct ecclesiastical word was) for the elderly and beloved Regenmacher.

Declan shook his head. "I've never been a parish priest. A bit of a professional stretch." He shrugged. "But it's what's on offer. Take it or leave it."

My shock at his suddenly bitter tone must have been clear on my face, for Declan continued:

"One takes holy orders to serve God, the Church, and one's fellow man—not oneself. But one is only human, after all."

"I'm sorry, Declan," I said, meaning it.

"Thank you. Mother would have admonished me for my lack of faith in God's plan. How she kept hers will always be a mystery to me."

I sat on the sofa while Declan prepared cocktails at the old-fashioned drinks trolley in the adjacent dining room. It was the only furniture in the once cluttered room, and I wondered where we were going to eat.

"I saved this for you," said Declan, tapping the trolley with his foot. "Mother knew how much you admired it. She wanted you to have it."

"That was sweet of her. Thank you."

Declan returned with two martinis and sat down beside me. "Cheers," he said, raising his glass.

"To Elspeth." I took a sip. Delicious. Declan might have had his doubts about his pastoral skills, but his mixology was on point. "You know," I continued, "if the parish priest thing doesn't work out, you can always fall back on bartending."

Declan laughed. I wondered how long it had been since he'd done that.

"How are you holding up?" he asked

"In a nutshell, everything hurts."

"And your memory recovery?"

"Well, it seems to be improving. The disorientation is gone, that feeling of living someone else's life that's hung around for the last few weeks. But I've got a way to go. And I need to face the fact that some of my memories may never return."

Declan's eyes narrowed, and he nodded slowly. He, of all people, could understand how I felt, having observed his mother's losing battle with dementia.

"You're in good hands," Declan said. "I'm told Dr. Malhotra is the best. Actually, it was Mother's specialist who recommended her."

"Recommended? What do you mean?"

"Recommended her to Mr. Summerly. Joshua was aware of my situation, of course, and he asked me for advice about brain doctors. I put him in touch with Mother's physician, and he, in turn, recommended Wending Hills and Dr. Malhotra."

I felt ashamed of myself. I never gave a thought to how I'd ended up at Wending Hills. My insurance paid for it; that was all that concerned me. Joshua, the Good Samaritan, never mentioned his involvement. I'd assumed the hospital had made the arrangements. I owed him big time. And I owed a debt of gratitude to Declan, as well.

"I had no idea," I muttered. "Thank you, Declan."

"It was nothing, Cal. You made a good call naming Joshua as your healthcare proxy. The man isn't nearly as airheaded as he pretends."

That made me laugh. Though it dawned on me, as I took another sip of my martini, that I was sleeping with the enemy, as it were. Having cocktails with the man I blamed for Paul's religious conversion. However, I was also seeing Declan in a new light. I had always thought of him as Paul's friend, even though I interacted with him frequently at the community center. Now, I understood he was my friend too. The realization disturbed me. What else had I got wrong?

"Are you hungry?" Declan asked.

"You did invite me to dinner," I responded, sniffing the air for telltale signs of our impending feast.

"Sorry. Not here. I just about manage to burn the occasional slice of toast."

"Join the club."

"I was thinking about The Soundview."

Of course. Aside from the little Thai gem off the green on Main Street, The Soundview was the only decent restaurant in town. Hell, it was the only decent restaurant this side of Fairfield. Plus, as its name correctly implied, the main dining room afforded a panoramic view of Long Island Sound. And, if memory served, the grilled prawns were fabulous.

"Sounds great," I said. "But..." I glanced pointedly at our nearly empty glasses.

"No worries. Reggie can take us."

"Reggie?"

"Reggie. The taxi driver."

"Guns and Roses," I said.

"The very one. You remember him?"

"Not really. Although, I felt comfortable enough with him to let him drive me from the station to my house, so I guess he's inside somewhere." I tapped my temple for emphasis.

"Right, then. How about you top us up while I change and put in a call to 'Guns and Roses.'"

"Done deal, Padre."

*

The town of Hollyford might have been liberal in its voting record, but apparently, the sight of two men dining in a romantic, candlelit setting could manage to raise the odd eyebrow. No eyebrow could have been odder than the one arched on the cosmetically distorted face of the elderly gentleman seated diagonal to Declan and me as we sat perusing our menus.

"I know I've seen that old man somewhere before," I whispered to Declan, tilting my head in the man's direction under cover of my raised menu. "But I can't remember where. He's a dead ringer for the late Duchess of Alba."

Declan chuckled softly. "Without the frizzy hair... Yes, you're quite right," he said. "Leonard Gottschalk. He's one plastic surgery away from a complete monstrosity. He's also on the board of the Bingham. The one dissenting voice against the mounting of your exhibit last year. Considered it pandering to the 'homosexual agenda.'"

"Of course," The Lego pieces snapped together. "The idiot who accused me of being a 'corrupting influence upon the moral fiber of Hollyford.'"

"Got it in one," replied Declan. "However, he's also a major contributor to the Church of St. Cecelia Preservation Fund." Declan turned toward the elderly man and his female companion, smiled warmly, and inclined his head with pontifical grace.

"Do you realize what a hypocrite you are, Father Mac Graith?"

"Of course," replied Declan, once again scrutinizing the menu. "The skirt steak looks good. What are you thinking about?"

"That I hardly know you, Declan."

Gottschalk and his lady friend departed sometime between the arrival of our appetizer and main course, lightening the atmosphere considerably with their absence.

"Well," I said after the couple had made their exit. "You probably won't be earning a merit badge from the 'Duchess' after being seen consorting publicly with the Mapplethorpe of Hollyford."

"Consorting? No. Ministering to a parishioner, colleague, and prominent member of the community. I believe Gottschalk developed a taste for crow after the success of your exhibit. Really, he can hardly consider himself an art connoisseur if he has a problem with the occasional phallus."

I'd told Declan that I hardly knew him, and it was true. Impaired memory or not, I was certain I'd never engaged in a conversation such as this with him. Had I even known he had a sense of humor? I found myself smiling. I was enjoying myself. Not at all what I had anticipated. I recalled Malhotra's advice about letting go of anger and stepping away from placing blame. Maybe she had a point.

Over the main course, our conversation drifted to a discussion of art and eventually led to my work at the community center.

"Melody sends her regards," said Declan. "Expect a call in the next day or so. I told her you need time to reacclimate." He cut a slice of rare steak. "Are you sure it's not too soon? You seem to be recuperating rather well, but, even so..."

"I think I'm ready. It might be more of a physical challenge than I imagine; I might need to cut the class time down. But I must get back to work. My brain needs the exercise as much as, or more than, my body. And I have the imprimatur of my visiting medico." I explained to Declan about Duguay.

"Oh, yes. The handsome, curly-haired young man I spied walking up your front steps as I was pulling weeds and otherwise minding my own business."

Like mother, like son.

I smiled and skewered a shrimp. "Declan." I was intrigued by the wording of his last sentence. "Are you gay?"

"Happy, content for the most part. But gay? Rarely. Why do you ask?"

"Oh, come off it," I said. "You know what I mean."

"I am homosexual, Cal. To be gay, I would have to be an active member of the team, which, of course, is frowned upon by Holy Mother Church."

"You mean, you never..."

"Not since my ordination. Believe it or not, many of us do take the vow of celibacy seriously. It's about focus, rechanneling physical desires to concentrate that energy on spiritual growth."

I sipped my wine as I considered my next question.

Oh, what the hell. Go ahead, ask. He probably expects you to.

"And you don't ever...?" I surreptitiously made the universal gesture for male masturbation.

"Really, Calixto!"

"Sorry."

I returned my attention to my food.

Then, Declan laughed and slapped the linen-covered tabletop.

"Lord Almighty," he declared. "Your rueful expression is priceless. Particularly since you've never struck me as the type who does rueful. So, I'll throw you a bone—no, bad choice of words—I'll offer you a concession. The answer to your question is yes. I did admit to being human, remember?"

It was the opening I'd been waiting for. At the risk of ruining a pleasant evening, I said, "Speaking of celibacy, I need to talk to you about Paul."

"Ah." Declan picked up his wine glass and swirled its contents.

"What does 'ah' mean?"

"It means I wondered how long it would take us to get to this. Look, Cal, I can understand that, from your point of view, I may seem to have had some influence over Paul's decision to enter the Church, but you must understand the decision was his and his alone. Paul did seek me out for counsel—as a friend. I was not his spiritual advisor in any formal sense."

"You pulled strings for him, though, didn't you? Your Vatican connection. I know the Catholic Church has a shortage of priests, nuns, and monks, but I can't see it actively recruiting from the ranks of the middle-aged."

"Your last observation is quite accurate. Only a few orders accept older novitiates. I helped guide Paul toward those I felt might be a good fit. Eventually, he chose to join the Lay Cistercians. There was no string pulling involved."

I didn't entirely buy the last part, but I felt inclined to accept the sincerity and honesty of the rest. Why shouldn't I have? What possible motive could Declan have to lie to me? The truth was, I had not driven Paul away, and Declan had not arranged for Paul to be spirited away in the night against his will. He'd simply supported Paul in his decision; something I had failed to do.

I recalled what Malhotra had said at the end of our last session.

"I know you understand, Cal. The thing is, I want you to know you understand."

I was beginning to.

"I believe I owe you an apology, Declan," I said.

Declan raised an eyebrow as he refilled my wine glass. "Whatever for?"

"For not making the effort to see things from your point of view."

Declan frowned as he slowly shook his head.

"Knowing you both socially, I ought to have been more prudent with respect to Paul's spiritual struggle, not become so personally involved. Talking with you has made me realize that. Actually, I've been struggling with the question of whether I should talk to you about this. It's been bothering me since Paul passed away. You see, Paul's initial intention was to become a novitiate, to pursue holy orders."

"I know."

"But I counseled against following that path. I did not believe it was right for Paul. His faith was strong, but..." Declan shrugged. "Paul seemed overeager—he wanted everything to happen overnight. I suppose part of that could have been put down to his age, but I couldn't help but feel there was more to it than that. As genuine as his devotion to God was, I was convinced he was looking to the Church as an escape from the world, from life."

"From me?"

Declan made a dismissive gesture. "Whatever relationship issues you and Paul might have had, it was clear to me that Paul loved you very much."

"Then, why?"

"Why is the sky blue, Cal? I'm not a psychiatrist. Paul told me he wanted to serve God. He was not the first, nor will he have been the last to leave his family and loved ones to pursue a calling."

"That's not fair."

"Cal—"

"I know, I know. Life isn't fair."

"That's not what I was going to say, but it's also difficult to argue with."

"I'm sorry, Declan. You were a good friend to Paul. You and I have been colleagues for almost two years. I think it would be nice if we could be good friends as well."

"I'd like that."

The chip on my shoulder finally slid off and shattered on the floor. The ease of it was surprising—and mildly unsettling. I've never been comfortable with things that are too easy.

I chose to ignore my suspicion that there was something Declan wasn't telling me.

Chapter Five

"My, aren't we ambitious!"

Such was Joshua's comment when I informed him that I intended to hold a dinner party the following week. My last encounter with Duguay had emboldened me, spurred me to get back into the swing of things. Intimate gatherings of friends had been a staple of my old life with Paul, and I'd worked myself up to the challenge of making them a part of my new, single life.

"Well," I replied," cradling the slimline phone on my shoulder as I flipped once again through the Nigella Lawson cookbook. "I'm counting on you for culinary support."

"So, you want me to play Sue Ann to your Mary? Darling, you know how I loathe typecasting."

"Oh, really? Then don't call me Mary."

"Well, you *can* turn the world on with your smile."

"Joshua, stop before I vomit over Nigella."

"Bless you for that visual. Of course I'll help you with your little gathering. I've got a decent break before that damned summer festival I should never have agreed to. Fancy a houseguest?"

I recalled my conversations with Duguay and Declan and the references to Joshua's kindness and concern.

"Thank you, Joshua. For *everything*," I said, barely holding back tears.

"What are you on about? I'll help you shop. We can pick up everything at Balducci's in Westport. Of course, we *won't* be preparing veal Prince Orloff, but—"

"I didn't mean—"

"I know."

"I love you, Joshua."

"Don't go getting all misty-eyed. Crying ages one. Not that you have anything to worry about, you creaseless Latina bitch."

I smiled as I closed the cookbook. "Okay. So, Thursday? Friday? Declan and Melody are good with either."

"Which day does the delectable Duguay visit?"

"Thursday. I never said he was delectable."

"I shall arrive Wednesday evening. Make certain all is in order."

"*A presto.*"

I hung up, and then the phone rang again thirty seconds later.

"What about Barbie and Ken?" demanded Joshua.

"Huh?"

"Thor and Freyja. Your neighbors with the two kids—one adorable munchkin and one ice queen in training."

"Oh, I hadn't thought about them," I lied. I hadn't thought about much else.

"Well, you and Paul were rather close with them, I thought. They might feel insulted if you don't invite them. Sans offspring, of course."

"Whose party is this anyway? Okay. You're probably right."

"Of course, I am. Let me know if they accept. Ciao."

Click.

So much for indecision. I took a deep breath and dialed Eric's number. Jill answered after two rings. I was batting a thousand.

"Cal, how nice to hear from you! Eric told me all about your accident. I'm *so* sorry I haven't been over to say hello, but you know how insane my schedule is."

Blah, blah, blah.

"Don't worry about it," I said, trying to mimic the artificial warmth in Jill's voice. "Joshua's been to visit, and a nurse comes three times a week just to make sure I'm not lying dead on the kitchen floor."

"Oh..."

"I'm kidding. Anyway, I'm planning a dinner party for next Thursday. I'd love for you and Eric to come."

"Thursday? Um...yes. Thursday's good for me. I'm sure Eric is free as well."

Because he has nothing better to do, Jill's tone seemed to imply.

"Great—7:30?"

"Perfect. Thanks, Cal."

"See you then."

That was that.

All right, Nigella. So, what does one prepare for a few friends, your neighbor, and her husband whom you've been fucking behind her back? Something in that smirk of yours tells me you must know...

*

There was a full moon that night. Perhaps it beckoned to me, or perhaps I just couldn't sleep. Either way, I found myself stretched out on the settee in the sunroom—more appropriately, the moon room—observing a cadre of opossums cavorting under the oak tree. The song "Dancing in the Moonlight" flitted through my mind, and I smiled despite the rather creepy effect of the lunar glow upon my garden. The entire space appeared as if viewed through a blue-black lens, even the various colors of the roses reduced to a common darkness, like cardboard flowers in a shadowbox. The opossums, not the cutest of animals in daylight, were disproportionately large and sinister in this nighttime tableau.

Yet, it was beautiful in its way, like most things if you look hard enough and don't think too much. The voice of one of my favorite professors from my college days popped into my head: "Let go of preconceived notions. See what you *see*, Calixto, not what you've been conditioned to *perceive*."

I shook my head, still impressed by the vagaries of art and art instruction. I'd spent hours, days, years working to master the mathematic principles and rules of art. Then, having finally been judged proficient, I'd been called out for not being able to throw those rules out the window. Finally, I realized painting was like poetry; rules couldn't be broken to good effect if they were never fully understood, and true understanding could not come until the rules were broken.

Could the same be said of life? Did playing by the rules limit you? Did it take a break from those rules to show you what life was about? Or did it take a brush with death?

I thought of Paul and his decision to leave the world as I knew it. As *we* knew it. Thus far, I hadn't been able to feel anything but anger and betrayal. But there, in the moonlight, watching the opossums, I sensed a glimmer of understanding. I still felt that Paul was an asshole for leaving me, but...it wasn't really *me* he left, was it? Maybe it wasn't so much a "leaving" as a "going to."

I began to cry. The opossums kept dancing.

*

I was cool, distant, when Duguay arrived on Saturday. I must have been giving off bad juju in spades, because Duguay responded to my mood immediately. There was none of our usual presession banter; everything was strictly business.

"I'm sorry," I said quietly as Duguay tapped away on his ThinkPad.

Duguay paused in his typing and looked up. "Not one of your better days, is it?"

"No."

Since my night under the moon, I'd felt glum and out of touch. No, that was wrong. I'd felt glum and *in touch*. And I wasn't thrilled with what I was touching. I'd been a slut, a schmuck, and had cast my partner as the fall guy. I was beginning to see rather than perceive. Or so it seemed.

"Thinking about what you told me yesterday? Paul...your *entanglement*?" Duguay asked.

I nodded.

"Perfection is overrated," said Duguay, lowering the lid of his laptop. "Striving for it only damages us in the end."

"Is that a quote?"

"Not that I'm aware. It does sound like one, though, doesn't it? Like something from a wall plaque or a T-shirt. I think the idea is valid, regardless of its origin. We can only try to do our best, and what 'best' is varies from person to person."

I turned this over a few times in my mind, then delivered my own quote:

"'I promise to do my best, to do my duty to God and my country, to help other people, and obey the law of the pack.'"

Duguay smiled. "So, we're fellow ex–Cub Scouts, I see."

"My mom was a den mother. Resistance was futile. But I never made it past wolverine, or whatever the first level is called."

"What a shame," said Duguay, his voice deadpan. "You missed out on the circle jerks."

I laughed, though I wasn't entirely sure Duguay was joking.

"That's more like it," said Duguay. "I wasn't digging Sad Cal."

Before I could pursue the "digging," Duguay continued:

"The Boy Scout pledge sounds hokey, but it's not a bad rule for living. It's a promise to *try*, not an unobtainable absolute."

"I memorized it—obviously," I said as I poured our coffee. "But I never really considered what it meant. Do they still do the pledge today?"

Duguay shrugged. "I have no idea. It's been years since I even *thought* about the Scouts. I enjoyed it, but I didn't make any lifelong friends."

"Despite the one-handed bonding?"

A slight widening of Duguay's candid eyes told me he hadn't been joking.

He sipped his coffee.

"Because of it, actually."

He set his cup down on the table. "I was a bit... um...how shall I put it? Overeager?"

"Ah," I replied, understanding completely. "If you look, it's okay. If you touch, you're a faggot."

"Essentially, yes."

We continued to drink our coffee in silence, and I felt closer to Duguay than I had to anyone since I met Joshua.

Interesting. Not: Since I met Paul.

"So," I said as Duguay polished his glasses with a slip of black cloth, "what's the plan for today?"

"The beach."

"The beach?"

"Yes. I've been studying a map of Hollyford. Walk right down Main Street, pass the train station, and continue on until you hit Hollyford Shores—and the beach."

"That's a *hell* of a long walk, Duguay."

"You're up to it," he replied. "Plus, there's a place called Mother Inman's Fish and Chips near the beachside. I love fish and chips. Is this place any good?"

I made a noncommittal noise. In fact, I'd not forgotten that Mother Inman's was one of my guilty pleasures. I recalled stopping by the popular local dive on many occasions to top up my RDA of fat and cholesterol after classes at the center.

"Well, then," said Duguay, rising and slipping his laptop into his briefcase. "Shall we have a go at it?"

*

There wasn't much of a beach to speak of. It was natural and picturesque, most of it a protected sanctuary for the wildlife that lived between the shore and the narrow marshland abutting the artery of I-95. But it was too narrow to draw a sunbathing crowd or waterside revelers. Even on a summer Saturday, it was deserted and felt more like a private retreat than a municipal public space. Yet, less than three-quarters of a mile north along the coast was a manicured bay with a large beach and a vast emerald-green lawn stretching toward the exclusive enclave of Hollyford Shores. From there, brief bursts of laughter, children's shrieks, and pop music carried over intermittently on the breeze only to be lost to the sound of the water or the cries of the seabirds.

"Why the beach?" I asked Duguay.

We removed our shoes, rolled up our pants, and proceeded to stroll. I'd assumed the sand would be a challenge, but the softness and warmth were delicious, and I hitched my cane in the crook of my elbow.

"Selfishness, mostly," he said, looking out at the Sound. "Many people find the environment therapeutic, so I can write it off as part of your treatment. But...really, I just wanted to see your piece of the shore." He turned to me. "You like it here, don't you?"

How could he know?

"Yes, but..."

"I'm not psychic, Cal. Call it intuition."

As I swung my left arm as we walked, it brushed Duguay's right. Our fingers touched and then entwined. It was such a natural gesture I barely contemplated its significance as we moved along the beach. It felt right. That was all there was to it.

"I spent most of my childhood in Chicago," Duguay continued. "Never saw the ocean. When my parents changed careers, we moved to Florida. To a beachside condo. I hated it at first. I'll never forget my first night, listening to the sound of the surf, harsh and cruel-sounding to my city boy ears.

"Then, one night, I was listening to the radio and picked up a signal from a station on the island of Bonaire. The program was about the night and the sea and the beauty of the ocean. It touched something inside me, and the sounds of the ocean ceased being scary and became a lullaby…a siren song, I guess you could say. I fell in love with the ocean then, and that love has never left me." Duguay's fingers squeezed mine. "I feel we have something in common. I don't know…maybe I'm wrong."

I did not respond.

"It's your artwork," he said, answering my unspoken question. "Not just the medium, but the colors—almost always shades of blue and green—and the… I don't know what you call it. I know nothing about art…the *style*, I guess. There's always this sort of undulation to everything, a constant movement. Every time I look at one of your paintings, even if it's one of two people making love, I can't help but think of the ocean…of…of *churning* life."

Jesus.

He got me.

He got my work.

I'd been somewhat cagey about my paintings since my first public exhibition, never liked to talk about "inspiration." I hated the intrusion. My website, which is where Duguay must have learned about my work, was bare bones, just the paintings and a buy link. I guess that was why my success as a painter had been so limited and had always taken a back seat to my career as a costume designer.

"You're very gifted," said Duguay softly.

"Thank you. I'm proud enough to acknowledge my talent, but 'gifted' is for saints and geniuses."

Duguay let go of my hand and turned his gaze to the Sound.

"We've all been given a gift, Cal. The trick is recognizing it and learning how to use it."

We walked along in silence for what seemed like forever.

"I'm not sure I have," I said eventually. "Learned, I mean. I'm not even sure if I know what my gift is."

"Well, you've given me a gift today. I've never shared that story about the sea with anyone until now. I don't know why, really. I guess I felt it was something very private, a place I went to alone when I needed comfort. But now I've told you, it feels *right*—as if the memory was just waiting to be shared with the one person who could understand it. That was your gift to me."

I had no idea what to say to that, but Duguay hardly gave me the chance to come up with something. He dropped his shoulder bag onto the sand and then began to strip.

"What the hell...?"

"Unfortunately," said Duguay as his shirt fell away to reveal smooth, pale skin and a lean, muscular torso, "I didn't bring a bathing suit." He began to unbuckle his belt, and I turned my head.

"Are you insane?" I demanded.

"Come on, Cal. It's just you, me, and the sea."

"It's Long Island Sound. I don't think it's technically the sea."

"It's *part* of the sea. Come *on*. It'll be great for improving your balance. And there's a natural barrier reef out there, you know. The water should be clean and fresh. Relatively speaking."

I turned back to the sight of Duguay, a feast for my eyes in square-cut black briefs, smiling and beckoning.

Suddenly, the possibility of getting arrested didn't seem so important.

"Come on, Cal. Get a move on!"

Duguay turned and waded into the surf.

"I'm not wearing any underwear," I called back.

"I'll keep my eyes averted until you're in waist deep. Okay?"

Fuck it.

I stripped clumsily but completely. More aware and unsure of my nakedness than I'd been since I was an adolescent, I followed Duguay into the water with cautious steps, laughing to myself as I imagined what Dr. Malhotra would make of all this. I moved unsteadily over rocks and shells and the weight of the water pushed against my body.

"I'm right here," said Duguay, offering a supportive hand that gripped mine and then slipped away to find purchase on my hip. I turned toward him, the current making the movement fluid. His face was close to mine, and I smelled his hazelnut-scented breath mixed with the aroma of sea and the unique fragrance of his skin and hair.

"Duguay, I..."

I never finished the sentence. A familiar voice called from the beach, intruding on the dreamlike quality of the moment.

Damn.

"I simply *must* engage a visiting nurse," said Joshua as he made his way toward us. He wore white linen trousers and a matching dress shirt, untucked, the sleeves rolled up to expose his hairy forearms. Over his right shoulder, he held a wood and paper parasol painted in an Oriental motif. I recognized the parasol as a prop I'd stolen from a regional production of *Anything Goes* and given to Joshua as a birthday present.

"Joshua!"

"Good afternoon, Mr. Summerly," added Duguay.

"Darling, please!" replied Joshua, addressing Duguay. "You can't possibly expect to pull off such a formal greeting when you and my dearest friend are wading in the water like Jesus and John the Baptist. Do call me Joshua. And you, of course, must be Marc." He glanced at our discarded clothing, then back at us. "Speaking of the Bible, a van pulled in next to my vehicle in the parking lot. It's sporting a Praise the Lord bumper sticker. I suggest you boys clothe yourselves posthaste."

We made our way back to the beach, Duguay supporting me for speed and safety, then fumbled wet into our clothes as Joshua stood guard, providing cover with his parasol and Duguay's lab coat. I was a fool. A happy fool, but a fool nonetheless.

Joshua looked us over, shaking his head and laughing.

"Not now, Joshua," I said. "Let's go, before the—"

"Oh, relax, Cal," Joshua drawled. "There is no van full of zealots. I made that up."

"You bastard."

"It was worth the risk of calling down your wrath just to see the look on your face." Joshua turned to Duguay. "My apologies to you, Nurse Practitioner, but I must say your hand-caught-in-the-cookie-jar expression was equally priceless."

Duguay laughed good-naturedly, which didn't surprise me. I suspected there was something of the trickster in him as well as in Joshua.

"I know you weren't expecting me until Wednesday, but I was overcome with an urge to escape from the island of Manhattan, and I pictured you, dearest Cal, all alone and forlorn in your cottage—like Mole lost in the Wild Wood. I thought, 'Go to him. Rescue him.' Imagine my surprise when I arrived at your abode and found only little Margarita toiling away."

Little Margarita, my housekeeper, was a statuesque, Eastern European graduate student next to whom I felt like Weakling Smurf.

"The estimable Marge informed me that you left a note saying you'd gone to the beach. So, of course, my curiosity was piqued." Joshua swept a look over Duguay. "And now that it's been satisfied"—he looked back to me—"how about lunch?"

"We were planning on stopping by Mother Inman's on the walk back."

"Walk? Are you mad? And you'll have to go home and change—or at least dry out, first."

"I'd appreciate the lift," interjected Duguay, "but I think I'd best just grab my briefcase from Cal's place and be on my way."

"Duguay—"

"No, really, Cal. I don't want to intrude. Plus, I've got a pile of paperwork waiting for me at home."

"Are you sure?"

Duguay nodded.

"Next time?"

"Absolutely."

He smiled, and I felt the butterflies again.

*

"Well, well, well."

Joshua made this irony-laden three-word pronouncement as he stirred the ice in his scotch and looked at me with a supercilious expression.

We sat alone in the mudroom after saying farewell to Duguay and Margarita, the latter having taken the former in hand and sent him on his way dry and pressed before taking her own leave.

I sipped my martini and waited for Joshua to elaborate, which he did presently.

"He's a very good-looking boy."

There was no ignoring the slight emphasis on the last word.

"Since when does thirty-something qualify as a boy?"

"Since you turned fifty, darling."

"Thank you *so* much for that."

Joshua smiled. "But you do see my point?"

"What? Just a few days ago, you were encouraging me to think of someone other than Paul."

"*Think*, yes. Cavort naked in public, no."

"It wasn't like that."

"Really? So, how was it, exactly?"

I drank deeply of my cocktail, then proceeded to describe the events of the day, my growing attraction to Duguay, our easy intimacy, and my suspicion that Duguay shared my feelings.

"Good Christ!" Joshua declared as he set his tumbler down with a thud. "I had no idea it was as bad as that."

"We're not discussing a terminal disease, Joshua."

"No. But it's just as dangerous. Firstly, he's your *nurse*. Secondly, you're in a very vulnerable state, not only because of the injuries to your body and your memory, but also to your psyche. Love on the rebound might work in the cinema or on stage, but in the real world, it seldom does."

I looked down at my glass, accepting the wisdom of Joshua's words while resenting them with equal measure.

"I saw the way you looked at him," continued Joshua in a softer voice. "I saw the way he looked at you. And what I see could be trouble."

"Thank you, Madame Blavatsky."

"I'm serious, Cal."

I don't know if it was the gin and vermouth or Joshua's condescending tone that did it, but anger welled up in me like lava from a previously dormant volcano.

"Will *anyone* ever be good enough for you, Joshua?" I demanded hotly.

"I—"

"Let me finish. You never approved of Paul, did you? From the beginning, you said he wasn't right for me. Then you bided your time waiting to be proved correct. Which, of course, you were. You haven't gloated—that's not your style—but you've let the implication hang. Now, all I had to do was speak from my heart about the mere *inkling* of feelings for someone new, and you immediately set out to poison my mind against him."

"*Poison your mind*? You're being melodramatic."

"Am I?"

Joshua looked out through the open French doors, his gaze seemingly fixed on some far distant point.

"I love you, Calixto. You've been my closest friend and confidant for more than twenty-five years. I'd be lying to myself and to you if I said that I never wondered what it might have been like if our relationship had taken a different direction all those years ago. And, yes, I've sometimes been jealous of the men who've shared your intimate life. But I would never stand between you and your dreams, your happiness. However, it *is* my duty, as a friend who cares deeply for you, to point out when I think you might be on the verge of making a complete ass of yourself."

Joshua turned his face back to me, his eyes glistening.

"I'm sorry, Joshua," I murmured, unsure what else to say—if there was anything else to say.

A half-smile appeared and disappeared on Joshua's lips.

"You're a most unconvincing liar. Of course, you're not sorry. Why should you be? You spoke your mind. I spoke mine. We've been honest with each other just as we've always been. There's no 'sorry' about it."

We finished our drinks, and I fixed another for both of us. Bruno whined piteously from the other side of the door leading to the kitchen, and I let him out. He ignored Joshua and me, cantering down the steps to settle himself in the rock garden.

"You're right about Duguay," I said finally. "Thank you for bringing me down to earth."

Joshua sighed. "Must everything always be so black-and-white to you? Life is not a costume shop." Joshua took a drink of his scotch, then elaborated. "Angela Ferguson told me— You must remember Angela? From the time we worked together on *Tosca* at the Met? Good. Well, Angela told me that you once went into a rant about work being done half-assed. The talk around the shop was that, with you, it was 'whole ass or no ass.' They referred to you as 'Whole Ass Restrepo.'"

Feeling both embarrassed and nostalgic, I laughed at the reminder of a past that seemed simpler and funnier in retrospect than it had ever been.

"My point is," continued Joshua, "that I think Marc might be good for you. Just take it slow. Don't run off a cliff like a lemming."

"Point taken."

We lapsed into silence again, each given over to his own thoughts. Eventually, I stretched out my left leg and nudged Joshua with my bare foot.

"I love you too."

Chapter Six

While Joshua's early arrival was a welcome surprise, his larger-than-life presence often irritated me as much as his love and support warmed me. Recalling what Duguay had told me about Malhotra's proposal to Joshua that he stay with me for a few weeks during my recovery—and his subsequent refusal—I began to wonder if this fussy, mother hen behavior of his wasn't some sort of do over, a balm to his conscience.

Or was it his way of putting a wedge between me and Duguay?

Intentional or not, Joshua's company put a damper on the closeness I believed was developing between Duguay and me.

Duguay's visits on the following Monday and Tuesday lacked any of their earlier charm. He was pleasant, professional, and distant. The subject of our proposed fish and chip lunch was never broached. Joshua left Duguay and me to our own devices during our sessions, but his presence was still felt keenly in his absence. It was one of his gifts as an actor to always be present in a scene even when his character was offstage. It made me nervous and jumpy for no good reason and more sensitive to my semi-invalid state. I felt like Blanche Hudson in *What Ever Happened to Baby Jane*. I could just hear Joshua's voice:

But ya'are in a wheelchair, aren't ya Blanche?

I laughed aloud at my flight of fancy—as much at the ridiculousness of the idea as at the vision of Joshua costumed as Jane, shuffling around my house plotting and scheming, ordering large quantities of alcohol from the local liquor store (he *did* do that, actually), and serving me dead rats on a silver tray.

"Whatever is the matter with you?" asked Joshua, taking the three-pound package of fresh rabbit meat from the counter man and placing it in our shopping cart. "One minute you're scowling and snitty, the next you're giggling like the village idiot."

We were at Balducci's, shopping for my big dinner the following evening. Physically, I was feeling good, stronger—thanks to Duguay's deceptively simple regimen of walking, yoga, and free weights. I rarely stooped, tripped infrequently, and relied less and less on the cane for balance. My body was recovering. But I had doubts about my mind. My nights were plagued with bizarre dreams and my days with self-doubt about my relationships with Paul, Eric, and even Joshua. About my life, in general. I understood that nothing would be the same as before, but I had difficulty getting a grip on the possibilities of the future. Too many things about the past were unclear. As much as I wanted to embrace Joshua's advice and simply let go and move on, I found that nothing was simple, and moving on emotionally was much more complex than getting my body back into shape.

"Predinner party jitters," I said evasively. It didn't matter. Joshua had already turned his attention to a review of our shopping list.

"Truffle oil!" Joshua exclaimed. "I almost forgot."

"You get on the line," I said. "I'll hunt down the fungus oil."

"Okay."

I watched as Joshua wandered off in the opposite direction of the checkout, wondering what else he would buy that wasn't on our list, then I moved off to fulfil my part of the bargain. As I turned the corner of the oil section, I came face to face with Belinda Lindstrom.

"Hello," I said. "My first time here in months and I run into someone I know. How small world is that?"

"You don't *know* me," she replied and turned away.

"Hey," I continued, "I was just being polite. Something you ought to try."

Belinda dropped her basket and turned back, anger flushing her beautiful face.

"You've really got some pair, haven't you?" she demanded. "Smiling and acting all friendly after what happened?"

"Belinda, I—"

"Look Cal." Belinda stepped closer. "I'm sorry about the accident, all right? Nobody deserves that. And he's the one I should be angry with, not you. But you could have stopped it, and you didn't. You could have stopped it, Cal."

Belinda's eyes welled with tears, and I looked on, speechless, as one dripped down her smooth, pale cheek. Then, she turned and fled, leaving her basket behind.

Damn.

Suddenly, I felt unsteady. Or maybe it was the room moving around me. I leaned heavily on my cane, put my left hand against the nearest shelf, and closed my eyes.

"Are you all right, sir?"

I opened my eyes to find a kid—a stock boy or something—looking at me with concern. Managing a smile, I said, "Don't worry; I won't die on your shift."

The kid opened his mouth as if to say something, but nothing came out. He just stared at me.

"Seriously, I'm fine. I appreciate your concern."

This got me a nervous twitch of the lips and duck of the head, and then the boy was off like a shot.

Eric had told me I had a way with kids. Yeah, right.

Eric. How the hell did Belinda know? We'd always been so careful.

At least, that was what Eric told me.

Shit and double shit.

"You look like shit," said Joshua, voicing my unspoken expletive as he approached with our overladen carriage. He looked toward the exit, then back at me. "Wasn't that the ice-queen-in-training who just flew past me like an avenging harpy?"

"Joshua", I said, laughing despite my mood. "What you just said makes no sense. I don't think harpies avenge anything."

Joshua shrugged. "You understood my meaning, didn't you?"

"Yes. And that *was* Belinda. Can we check out now?"

"Sure. Why don't you wait outside? Some fresh air will perk you up."

I nodded assent.

"But be a love and grab that truffle oil first."

*

"Do you think Jill knows?"

I shook my head. A gesture Joshua could not see as his attention was on the road ahead of us. But he must have sensed my head rattling.

"She wouldn't, would she?" Joshua continued. "Not if she accepted your dinner invitation. Well, not unless she's a *thorough* bitch."

"I believe that part's already taken," I mumbled, not feeling much better for my earlier parking lot confession to Joshua.

We drove on in silence for a while, and the quiet felt like a weight of condemnation rather than the absolution I'd hoped for.

"Well, what's done is done," said Joshua, providing a modicum of comfort. "And I've been there and done that myself, so I can't be too harsh a judge." Joshua paused as he shifted gears. "Mind you, my partner in adultery didn't have children, so you're the bigger sinner."

"Gee, thanks."

"What astounds me is that you still can't remember doing it. I mean doing *it*. Trust me, darling, if a man as well-endowed as Mr. Eric had been banging my bussy—"

"Your *what*?"

"Bussy. Boy pussy. Don't you look at *any* porn on the internet?"

I shook my head. I preferred to use my imagination.

And look where that got me.

"Anyway," continued Joshua, "if Eric had been hammering *my* hiney with that whopper of his, *I* would remember!"

I smiled and said, "Do you realize you lose your English accent when you talk dirty?"

"Really?"

"Yes. And your old Texas twang creeps in."

"I must watch that," said Joshua gravely, his Received Pronunciation restored.

According to Joshua's official bio, he had spent his "formative years" in England. Only an actor could stretch a three-semester stint at Cambridge into formative years.

"Surprisingly," I said, getting back on topic, "Belinda seems to put the blame squarely on Eric. Now I think of it, she seemed more disappointed in me than angry at me."

"Is that so strange?" asked Joshua as we pulled into my driveway. "If she was very close to her father, I imagine the shoe would be on the other foot. But, as far as I've been able to observe, she doesn't appear to have a very good relationship with him."

"I suppose you're right. It's just the words she used struck me as odd— 'He's the one I'm angry with, not you. But you could have stopped it.' So, she blames her father for initiating the affair, but blames me for allowing it to continue. That's a quirky distinction to me."

And somewhat inaccurate. But I chose not to belabor the detail. I hadn't shared with Joshua the fact that it was I who'd done the seducing. I felt I'd lowered myself enough in my friend's opinion for one day.

It wasn't until we'd finished unpacking our food and had begun to review the menu for the dinner party that I once more brought up the subject of Eric.

"It's Wednesday evening," I observed, opening a bottle of chardonnay.

"Very good, Cal," replied Joshua with mock enthusiasm. "I must ring Dr. Malhotra immediately and inform her of your miraculous progress."

I poured a glass of wine for Joshua. "Very funny. You see, Wednesday evening was our usual...um... rendezvous. Eric and me, I mean."

"Rendezvous is French for 'hookup,'" said Joshua, accepting his wine with a little nod.

"It is not. And it wasn't like that. Well, I don't *think* it was."

"Well, whatever it was, you can't intend for it to continue. Can you?"

"No. I mean, I don't think so."

"You don't *think* so?"

"It's difficult to explain."

"Try me."

"Okay. When I was with Eric the other day, the sex was fantastic. But I didn't feel connected emotionally. *He* was though. Joshua, I think Eric's in love with me."

"Christ."

"And *I* might have been in love with *him*. I just don't remember."

"What does your gut tell you?"

I stared at my wine for a while, thinking, the certainty of my feelings clearer now that I was discussing them with Joshua.

"He's a really nice guy and a great fuck. That's all. I can't believe my involvement with him went deeper than that."

Joshua gave a dramatic sigh. "That's sorted then," he said with a strong note of finality.

"Yes."

But it wasn't *sorted*. Not in my head. And I was only half of the equation. There was Eric to consider. Eric's feelings.

How could I have been so stupid?

I decided to channel my inner Scarlett O'Hara and think about it tomorrow.

But the dinner was tomorrow. The dinner that I was more and more certain would turn out to be a complete disaster.

*

"You big fat liar!"

It was hardly the greeting I expected.

Melody Lewis stepped back from her welcome kiss and stood with her hands planted on her ample hips. Her persimmon sweater dress, belted high under her bosom, did absolutely nothing for her figure, but she wore it with panache, defying anyone to tell her so.

"You look perfectly all right to me," she continued, giving me a once over. "Here I was, expecting to find a poor wreck in a wheelchair with his hair in need of a dye job."

"You know damned well that my hair color is natural."

"Of course, dear. We all have our little vanities."

I gave Melody my best resting bitch face, then smiled, glad I'd had the forethought to remove my stash of Color Silk from the linen closet in the guest bathroom.

"Seriously," said Melody, "I'm relieved to see you looking so good. I was worried."

There was scolding in those last three words, and I deserved it.

"I'm sorry, Melody. I should have called you sooner. Should have answered my students get well card sooner. There's no excuse."

"Honey, you almost died...and you're still dealing with the loss of Paul. I think a social faux pas here and there is allowed."

"Thanks."

I hugged Melody tightly, then led her through the cottage to the sunroom.

"Everyone *else* is here already," I said, allowing myself my own little scolding.

It was a balmy evening, so Joshua—enlisting the help of Declan—had moved the dining table to the garden and refashioned the sunroom as an indoor-outdoor drawing room. The French windows were thrown wide; allowing the fragrance of roses to drift in on a light breeze.

My guests occupied sofas and chairs, each seeming to have chosen one suited to his or her persona as well as shape and size. Declan, in clerical garb, sat prim and cross-legged in a Hepplewhite chair, looking every inch the village vicar. Jill reclined glamorously on a divan, her black halter-top jumpsuit the perfect counterpoint to the zebra-print upholstery. Making a convincing case for manspreading, Eric, in a muscle flattering red polo, occupied the leather sling chair like a porn star Santa Claus waiting for someone to sit on his lap. Melody chose a flower-shaped chair perfectly befitting her queenly proportions.

Declan had brought with him my new drinks trolley, and I moved behind it, ostensibly to prepare a cocktail for Melody but also thinking of the bar as a barricade behind which I could protect myself from the press of social interaction.

Pull yourself together, man.

As I mixed a Cuba libre, I was grateful for the distraction of observing Joshua, in a Kelly-green oxford, swan in from the garden and perch on the frame of Eric's chair, a bear-sized elf to Eric's Santa. I delivered Melody's drink, catching the glint of amusement in her eyes as she took in the tableau of Eric and Joshua.

"They make a cute couple, don't they?" she whispered. Then we both laughed, and I felt my tension ease a bit.

"What are you two giggling about?" demanded Joshua.

"We were just making a wager," replied Melody, "over which would break first on that chair—the leather straps or the aluminum frame."

Joshua raised an eyebrow. "Or if you'll need both of us to extricate you from your throne?"

Melody laughed and raised her glass to Joshua. Good-natured banter about their respective weights was long-established between them. Melody considered herself Rubenesque, while Joshua described himself as strapping.

Jill looked on, smiling, the indulgent size six beauty.

Declan smirked. "Isn't this the moment when you make a speech, Cal?"

"That's right," said Jill. "Like in a detective story— 'I know you're all wondering why I've asked you here this evening...'"

I suppose it was my guilty conscience, but something in her tone made me wonder if she really did know about me and Eric and was taking pleasure in toying with me in her role as wronged wife. She certainly looked the part, with her sleek updo and stiletto-heeled sandals.

"Oh, all right," I said, shaking off the gruesome thought. "But I need a martini first."

Declan did the honors, and as I raised my glass in a toast, I was aware of two things: I missed Paul, and I missed Duguay—in different ways, of course. I missed Paul's social ease. Missed the comfort of standing slightly in the shadow of someone confident in any situation, letting him take control. Conversely, it was Duguay's ability to make me feel like the center of attention that I missed. Well, like it or not, I was now the center of *everyone's* attention.

"Um..." *Great start, Calixto.* "I'm glad you could all come." *More brilliance.* "Sorry, this isn't easy." Murmurs of sympathy. "My idea was to have this party to mark a new beginning in my life. But, as someone recently pointed out to me, the past never goes away...it becomes part of us. So, rather than toast to a new beginning, I'm going to toast to a new way of living the same journey."

Not bad.

"Here, here," intoned Declan, at once congratulating me on my speech and indicating that I'd said enough.

Thank you, Declan.

"So, what, exactly, does this 'new way of living' entail?" Jill asked.

"Well, for starters, I've decided to get back to work," I replied, then turned my attention to Melody. "Work at the center, I mean. I'm giving up costume design for good to work full time as a teacher."

Melody smiled, but then her smile faltered. "Are you sure it's not too soon? Obviously, you're recovering just great. But is it wise to push yourself?"

A look passed between Melody and Declan. One of those "should you tell him, or should I" looks.

They've replaced me. Of course. It's been more than two months...

Melody must have read my mind.

"We'd be happy to have you back, Cal," she said. "And I'm all for expanding the curriculum...adding more classes. That would be *fantastic*."

But...

"But," continued Declan smoothly, "we need you at 100 percent." He smiled at Melody. "The center couldn't afford the bad publicity if you were to collapse on the job."

He said it with a laugh in his voice, but there was something tense, guarded in the look exchanged between Melody and him. I didn't like it, but neither did I understand it. I was about to let it pass when Eric added his two cents.

"They've got a point, Cal. You don't want to rush things and risk reversing all the progress you've made."

"True," agreed Jill.

Declan gave Jill an approving tilt of his head, as if thanking her for the backup.

Had they rehearsed this? A united front to help "poor Cal"? Feeling more bullied than cared for, I shot an inquiring glance at Joshua, who returned it with a don't-ask-me face.

I repressed ungrateful feelings and said, "I suppose you're right. Though my visiting nurse would probably disagree. I'm just feeling so damned squirrelly."

"What about a cruise?" suggested Jill, stretching catlike on her chaise. "Eric and I have been talking about taking one for *years*, haven't we darling?" She smiled sweetly at her husband.

"Yes. But with Jill's insane workload..." Eric shrugged, simultaneously complimenting and blaming his spouse.

You've learned from a mistress of subtle put-down, haven't you, Eric?

"Went on one with a group of girlfriends," chimed in Melody. "Hated every minute of it. I love each one of those ladies, but I'll be damned if they weren't the biggest bunch of cock blockers."

This comment elicited laughter all around, defusing a potential spat between Eric and Jill.

"Well, Cal," said Declan, poker-faced, "you could go on a gay singles cruise. It's my understanding that cocks are rarely blocked on such excursions."

All eyes turned to the priest, and a short, stunned silence was followed by another burst of laughter.

"I can't *wait* to hear your first official sermon, Father Mc Graith," said Joshua. "Congratulations, by the way, on your investiture...or whatever it's called."

"Thank you, Summerly. Consider yourself invited to the after-party."

"Cocks or no cocks," I said, getting belatedly into the groove, "I don't think a cruise is in the cards. I feel pretty good, but I'm not up to traveling on my own."

Joshua waggled his eyebrows. "You could take the delectable Duguay as a companion."

Melody sat up straighter. "Who is this 'delectable' Duguay?"

"Cal's visiting nurse," answered Joshua before I could open my mouth. "All Pre-Raphaelite curls and Caravaggio lips."

"Ooh..." said Melody. "What's the name of that agency?"

"I've already done the research for myself," offered Joshua. "I'll email you the link."

*

As the evening progressed, my apprehensions faded. Good food, good wine, and good company worked their magic. Jill and Eric seemed less thorny with each other than I remembered them, and I wondered again—less fearfully than before (my feelings mellowed by alcohol)— if indeed Jill knew about or suspected my liaison with her husband. If so, maybe theirs was an open marriage. Maybe Eric's dalliance had brought them closer together. Maybe I had been an agent of good rather than corruption. Things like that did happen, didn't they?

Yes. In Lifetime movies and telenovelas.

Talking myself into a belief in my inadvertent virtue, the inevitable after-dinner pairing off began. Large groups usually break into smaller ones, and sometimes, couples drift off or singles flit between groups. But our number was small and even, so choices were limited as we gradually moved away from the table to stretch our legs and enjoy the evening and the garden. Ever one for a challenge, Joshua buttonholed Declan—encouraged by his gay cruise comment, no doubt—and proceeded to vamp him. Melody, declaring herself "down with the swirl," latched onto Eric, leaving me with Jill.

"Do you mind if we go inside for a minute?" asked Jill as I refreshed her white wine, and then, leaning closer, "I need to speak with you privately."

This was it then, shit hitting the fan time.

"No. Of course not."

I led the way into the sunroom and made to continue farther inside the house, but Jill stopped me.

"Here is fine, Cal."

I eased myself into the corner of the chaise Jill had occupied earlier, and she sat down on the edge beside me.

Little Miss Muffet...

"I want to talk to you about Paul," Jill began, surprising me.

I felt a twinge of uncertain relief.

"And I want to tell you how sorry I feel."

"Sorry?"

"Yes." Jill sighed heavily, then took a sip of wine. "For making snap judgements about you and your relationship with Paul. Eric did warn me, but of course, I didn't listen. We've developed such a habit of disagreement over the years...well, you know..."

I did. Sort of. I certainly knew what it was to fall into relationship ruts and lose touch with what was really going on.

"Anyway," continued Jill. "As I got to know Paul, I got to know you in a way. I think Paul was a lucky guy."

What could I say to that? "Thank-you" would sound smug. I smiled instead—probably coming off just as smug.

"And Paul..." Jill hesitated, examining her wine. "I'm conflicted, Cal. I liked him a lot. We had so much in common. But the more I got to know him, the less I understood him. The way he left you—the reason— It made *absolutely no sense* to me. Sure, we weren't *that* close, but..." Jill shrugged. "Sorry, I'm not making myself clear."

"I think you are," I said. "People take sides when their friends' relationships end. It sucks."

"That's just it. I should be taking Paul's side, right? I mean, if I wanted to take a side. But I can't help feeling that he treated you badly. And I wasn't any better. The long and the short of it is that I'd like us to be friends. I can't begin to imagine how everything that's happened in the last few months has affected you—the accident, Paul's death. What happened in your life forced me to take a fresh look at myself...at my marriage. You see, Eric and I have decided to give it another shot."

"*Another*?"

Jill tilted her head and looked at me with her delicate eyebrows ever so slightly drawn together.

"Yes. For a while there, we were seriously thinking about getting a divorce...or a legal separation at least."

"I had no idea."

I hadn't really. At least, I didn't remember. All I could think about as Jill spoke was how relieved I was that she was apparently clueless of my affair with Eric. If Belinda kept her mouth shut, I'd be scot-free.

"But I'm sure you wouldn't have been surprised if we did. Given the way we carry on sometimes. Declan's mother always looked at me as if she were smelling something nasty...and I can only imagine the gossip around the neighborhood."

"It wouldn't have started with Elspeth." I came to the late woman's defense. She never struck me as the type, despite her over-the-fence indictment of Jill. Then again, with her dementia... "I recall many of our chats," I lied. "And she never had anything but nice things to say about you, Eric, and the girls."

You owe me one, Elspeth.

"That was an unfair insinuation on my part," said Jill. "The poor woman suffered enough."

Jill looked out at the other guests, all still well out of earshot, then back at me.

"There something else. I hadn't heard from Paul for weeks before the accident. It wasn't like him. We used to speak to each other at least a few times a week. The silence didn't feel right. I felt as if I'd done something to offend him. Did I, Cal? Did Paul ever say?"

I shook my head. From what I could remember, Paul and I had talked very little in the few months before his death. It hurt to know he'd spent more time in conversation with our neighbor than with me. Part of me wanted to resent Jill for her friendship with Paul; another part of me felt sad for both of us.

"No, Jill. He never talked about you. I guess your friendship was another part of his life Paul kept from me."

"I shouldn't have said anything. Shouldn't have asked. I'm sorry."

"Don't be. At least now I know I'm not the only one Paul shut out."

We finished our wine in silence while the rest of the group drifted back inside.

"You're meant to be the botany guide, Calixto," said Joshua, slipping an arm from around Declan's shoulder as they entered. "I don't know a tea rose from a tea dance. I'm certain I've been a well of disinformation for our dear pastor."

"A most entertaining well, nevertheless," replied Declan. "I don't think I'll look at a stamen the same way ever again."

"Jill, darlin'," said Melody, striding in behind Joshua and Declan, arm in arm with Eric. "Would you consider renting him out?"

"Believe me, I have given the idea some serious thought. But, in the end, I decided to keep him all to myself."

"Can't say I blame you."

"Nightcap, anyone?" I asked, rising and moving toward the portable bar. "Coffee?"

Jill accepted a refill of wine, but the others demurred.

"Thanks, Cal," said Melody. "But I think it's time I hooked up with my Uber driver."

"I, too, should be pushing off," added Declan.

I bade goodnight to Melody and Declan, exchanging the usual promises to call, and they departed via the garden. Jill and Eric shared the last of Jill's glass of wine, and were soon off as well. Joshua and I then sprawled in postparty relief.

"The food was excellent, as usual," I said, accepting Joshua's offer of one of his hand-rolled Indian beedis.

"Thank you, darling," replied Joshua on a plume of smoke. "So, now, the details!"

"Details?" I asked innocently.

"Don't be coy. You and the Ice Queen. No blood was shed, no hairs were pulled. What the hell did you two talk about?"

"Paul," I said. "And Eric. Apparently, the end of my relationship with Paul was a wake-up call for Jill and Eric. Divorce was avoided, and all is right with the Lindstroms."

"Except that you're still fucking Eric."

"Past tense."

"Sorry. Still, you're a damned lucky son of a bitch."

I gave a noncommittal grunt. "I'm not so sure." I said, putting the little cigarette aside, letting it burn out.

"You mean the avenging harpy?" Joshua shrugged. "Least said, soonest mended."

"Maybe you're right."

I relit my cigarette and we smoked silently for a few minutes.

"What *was* that look all about?" asked Joshua, out of the blue.

"What look?"

"The help-me-I'm-cornered look you gave me when the gang came down unanimously against you going back to work. I did return your look with a we'll-talk-about-it-later head tilt."

"Oh, sorry. I confused the gesture with a don't-ask-me. Our body language shorthand is getting rusty."

"That's not the only thing," replied Joshua sourly. "I spent my entire arsenal on Declan and not even a dent."

"Joshua, aside from being a man of the cloth, Declan's not even your type. He's most definitely a too-too-too."

There was some shorthand I couldn't forget. A "too-too-too" was a man Joshua deemed too tall, too white, and too skinny to be of any carnal interest.

"True. He does have a certain *something* though. It must be celibacy. You know, all that repressed sexual energy."

I refrained from sharing my knowledge of Declan's solution to that problem. Instead, I asked, "So, what do you make of it? Why are they all convinced I'm better off staying at home feeling sorry for myself rather than diving back into work?"

"Hmm...I'm not sure. Did you catch that little nod of approval Declan gave Jill?"

"Yes. I knew you'd spot it. It was as if they'd rehearsed the scene."

"I suppose there are three ways you can look at it. One, they're genuinely concerned about your health; two, they're—justifiably—concerned about your ability to function at the center. That you could, potentially, collapse or freak out or something."

"Seriously? And you said there are three ways. You only gave me two."

"The third way is the middle ground. They're concerned *for* you, but they are also concerned *about* you. People suffering from PTSD have been known to—"

"I am *not* suffering from PTSD. Oh, for Christ's sake, it's the curse of Wending Hills. They all think I'm a mental patient!"

"Well, *technically...*"

The unspoken words were plainly expressed by Joshua's ironic expression.

"Okay, okay. I get it. But it burns my ass, Joshua. It really burns my ass."

"I know, darling."

Joshua came to me and wrapped me in a bear hug.

"It gets better," he said soothingly.

"You're full of shit."

"And you wouldn't have me any other way."

"No. I don't suppose I would."

*

No one had liked the coffee.

I considered this as I sat on my swing, nursing a big mug of the freshly brewed beverage and recalling the events of Thursday evening.

Joshua had gone, off to a music festival in Perugia, and I was feeling his absence.

Not in a bad way though.

Liberated. That was how I felt. I could enjoy my coffee, my way, in my garden, and not give a damn what Joshua or anyone else thought about it.

"I think it might be a little bitter" had been Paul's stock response when I made the morning coffee. Not a total condemnation, of course. That was not Paul's way. But the criticism was clear.

Duguay, at least, enjoyed a good strong cup of java.

And Elspeth had, too...

Looking toward Declan's house, I recalled how entering the home had once been like stepping through a time vortex. Make that vortices. Every room seemed of a different period, from the Victorian parlor to the midcentury dining room to the 1970s kitchen. It was in the last that I sometimes found myself sitting with Elspeth, sampling her delicious baked goods and washing them down with black coffee. Elspeth's baking and cooking days were, apparently, her "good" days, and I was fortunate enough to share in some of them before her final decline made it impossible for her to enjoy her favorite pastime.

"Don't tell me your ma never baked a batch of cookies!"

Elspeth had said this as she offered me the nearly empty bowl in which she had mixed dough for Christmas cookies. I stared at it for a moment, wondering why she'd handed it to me. Then, assuming I was meant to do the washing up, I took it to the sink.

"You're supposed to eat it, not wash it away. You're a strange one, Calixto Restrepo."

Elspeth shook her head in disbelief, then turned away to remove a tray from the oven. When she looked back at me, I had a spoon in my hand.

She took it from me with an exasperated tut. "A spoon, for heaven's sake! What boy uses a spoon to clean the mixing bowl?"

I'm not a boy, Mrs. Mac Graith.

I nearly said it aloud, then realized that, at that moment, Elspeth might have believed I *was* a boy.

She confirmed my suspicions when she said, "Yes, you're a strange one. But you aren't nearly as peculiar as that gangly friend of yours with the unruly hair. Saw him mooning about your garden the other day, and he didn't half give me a fright." She patted her iron-gray bouffant as if the memory alone could have caused a strand to escape from its hair-sprayed cage. "It's what happens when they mature early, I suppose. Not quite right in the head, poor things."

I made a noise that could have been interpreted as agreement. Declan had explained to me how his mother sometimes confused the past and present. A "spell" could come on with no warning and pass just as abruptly.

"Bobby," continued Elspeth, wiping her hands with her apron. "Or maybe Brandon."

"Who, Mrs. Mac Graith?" I asked, feigning polite curiosity and hoping it wasn't a mistake to ask.

"No, I tell a lie. Your friend's name is William."

That pulled me up short. I did know a William, though I never thought of him as a boy. Perhaps Elspeth wasn't having a spell after all.

"Student would be the proper term, I suppose," said Elspeth. "More coffee?"

"Yes, thank you."

I safely assumed that Elspeth was referring to William Blake, my appropriately named, talented life drawing student from the center. He had the potential to become a truly great artist—and had the stereotypically moody personality to go along with it. Add to that his greater-than-average height, lanky bone structure, and his perpetually disheveled hair, and I suppose he could have given an unsuspecting elderly lady a fright. But he'd never been in my garden. He had, however, struck up a friendship with Declan and had once or twice visited my neighbor to borrow a book on stained glass or color theory. Elspeth was confused, but at least she wasn't delusional.

"William is a bit awkward," I allowed, as Elspeth poured. "And he certainly is mature for his age. Seventeen going on forty." I sipped my coffee and applied my index finger to the remains of the cookie dough. "But, then, all young people seem like that these days. The world's a different place than it was when we were their age."

Elspeth smiled at my inclusive phrasing.

"Don't go layin' it on, Cal. I'm nearly old enough to be your gran."

"Hardly."

Elspeth Mac Graith was in her late eighties. Not much older than my mother would have been if she were still among the living. Elspeth was nothing like my mother, but she was a kind, intelligent woman, and sitting in her kitchen filled with avocado-colored appliances transported me to distant, happy times.

Bruno brought me back to the present, barking and chasing after some small animal that had taken cover among the dwarf olives. A mouse, probably. Or a neighbor's cat. I drank the rest of my coffee, and my thoughts returned to William Blake. I'd forgotten about William. Strange how a memory of Elspeth had opened my mind to that of someone else.

William had realized a dream when he'd been accepted at Cooper Union, though his parents had balked, terrified at the thought of their only son alone in the Wicked City. I had done what I could to assuage their fears (well-founded though they were, I must admit), but it was the promise of a nearly full scholarship that ultimately brought them around.

A large, slobbering tongue licked at my bare toes, reminding me it was lunchtime for a certain member of my household.

"All right, all right. Five minutes. Okay?"

Bruno harrumphed, gave me a pathetic look, then slumped down onto the grass with his head between his forepaws.

"You've been taking drama lessons from Uncle Joshua, haven't you?" I demanded.

Bruno simply nuzzled further between his paws and gazed at me askance.

I cradled my empty mug, looking back at Declan's house, my mind's eye peering into Elspeth Mac Graith's kitchen, my thoughts once more reliving that coffee morning not so long past. An image of William Blake flitted by, and Elspeth's words replayed in my head.

"That gangly friend of yours... Saw him mooning about your garden the other day, and he didn't half give me a fright."

Why had Elspeth called him my "friend," then later corrected herself? And why—if Elspeth's memory hadn't been confused—had William Blake been "mooning about" in my garden?

Chapter Seven

For days, I'd hemmed and hawed about the talk I needed to have with Eric. But when Eric himself appeared on my doorstep, the time for prevarication came to an end.

"Whisky?" I asked.

Eric leaned against the kitchen island and regarded me through narrowed eyelids. I'd rebuffed his earlier attempt at a kiss, and he'd responded with a smirk, thinking I was playing hard to get, I suppose.

"Will I need it?"

"Maybe."

"Okay."

I poured a generous measure.

"Cheers," said Eric, raising the glass I handed him. "Jill told me she spoke to you about our divorce—or more precisely, the divorce we're not getting. I guess that's been on you mind?"

"Um..."

"Hey, I'm sorry, Cal. I meant to tell you about it the last time I saw you. Before the party, I mean. But...well, you and I were kinda busy with other stuff." Eric took a gulp of whisky. "And when you told me you didn't remember...I...I copped out. I figured it was better that way. You not knowing, not remembering."

"Not remembering *what*?"

"Everything."

I rubbed my forehead, then screwed my hair around with my fingers in frustration.

"Oh, for Christ's sake, Eric! Cut me a break and just *tell* me."

Eric took a deep breath and another swig of Teeling.

"It was all about custody of the kids," he said. "Of Susan, really. Belinda's almost legally independent. I spoke to a high-flying divorce attorney—recommended by a guy at my firm—and she told me the court would almost certainly find in favor of Jill. She said it might be possible to overturn the ruling if I could demonstrate I was in a committed relationship and could offer a stable home environment while Jill remained single and her career took precedence over childcare."

I cursed under my breath. "Tell me this isn't going where I think it is."

Eric set his drink down and crossed the room to embrace me. My instinct was to resist, but his gaze pulled me in and good sense forsook me.

"You were so good with Susan," he said softly. "And we were good together, you and me. It didn't seem impossible at the time. And it was clear that it was over between you and Paul. You know, Jill kept telling me she didn't understand how the two of you were a couple. I thought she was just being her usual judgmental self until I got to know you. Until I realized how miserable you were with Paul. How you deserved a new beginning as much as I did."

Eric kissed me, and I felt it. Felt that "sense memory" I'd been missing. I'd cared for this man. Cared deeply. I surrendered to the sensation of Eric's tongue sliding against mine, to the pressure of his hips, his erection pressing against my belly.

Then, I woke up.

"And now?" I asked, pulling away.

"Everything's different, Cal. While you were in the hospital, Jill and I...we worked things out. She said everything was her fault and asked me to forgive her." Eric brushed his hand over the stubble of his crew cut. "I didn't tell her about you. I mean, how could I? Then, when you came back, and we talked, and..."

Eric shrugged away further explanation. None was necessary. I'd been the possible means to an end, but I was no longer needed. Better still, I had no memory of the events. Eric stepped back, clearly seeing the anger in my eyes.

"Please, Cal. It's not how you think. We had something, you and me... It could have worked out. It's just that—"

"It's just that I nearly died, lost my memory, and Jill conveniently took that moment in time to beg your forgiveness. With my memory loss, I was out of the picture. Jill, by her admission of guilt, was back in it. You made the logical choice."

"Cal, listen, I—"

"No. I've heard enough. Obviously, everything's worked out perfectly. For you."

"Come on," Eric wheedled, moving close to me once more. "I still want you. I still need you—Even if I'm not free like I promised you once. I did what I did for my daughter; to keep her in my life." He took a gulp of whisky. "Look, Paul's gone. You don't have anything to feel guilty about anymore. We can—"

I turned away, repulsed by Eric's cavalier attitude and by my own complicity in the insane scenario he'd laid out. I felt ashamed of myself. Could I really have been so desperate for love and affection that I had acquiesced to such a ludicrous proposition? And now, Eric was using my amnesia as a quick fix, a way out. They say we get what we deserve. I suspected Eric and I were perfect examples of the truth of this aphorism.

"Please don't say any more, Eric. Let's just move on."

Eric reached out and stroked my hair with both hands.

"I loved you, Cal. I really did love you."

"I guess it should hurt me that you're talking in the past tense. But it's all past tense to me, right? Lucky you."

"Cal—"

"Goodnight, Eric."

I ushered a silent and shamefaced Eric through the foyer and out the front door.

Then, I returned to my kitchen and downed the remainder of his whisky.

*

It was like the classic sci-fi trope wherein a sinister computer or robot is tricked into overloading its circuitry by being bombarded with illogical questions and nonsense. That was the state of my mind as I sat up in bed, not drinking the Earl Gray tea I'd prepared and not reading the novel so highly recommended by Joshua. It was six o'clock in the morning. There was no use trying to sleep. Had I managed it, my dreams would certainly have been bizarre.

I took a long shower, carried the tea to the kitchen, dumped it, and made a large pot of coffee. I was hungry but lacked the energy or desire to do anything about it. I just sat there, drinking coffee and attempting to put my newly discovered memories in order, to square the reality they revealed about who I was with the person I'd thought I was.

Is this the unique perspective you hinted at, Dr. Malhotra? It sucks donkey dick.

Really, none of this is a surprise. You knew you had had an affair with Eric. Since it was more than just casual sex, shouldn't that make it easier to accept? Easier to justify? Less sordid?

It should have, but it didn't. I had to own my recollected feelings for Eric. I had cared for him. I still cared for him.

What the hell were you thinking, Calixto?

You knew going in that you were asking for trouble. And now you're pushing Eric away, making him the fall guy, washing your hands of him.

And you pushed Paul away too, didn't you?

Paul tried to take the blame. Turn the other cheek. And you let him. It was easier that way.

So much easier to hold on to anger than admit responsibility.

What is that theory Malhotra floated about everything being your own fault?

Is it true, after all? Or does it really take two to tango?

I was spared having to answer myself by the arrival of Duguay at precisely eight o'clock. I imagined him standing on my doorstep, eyes on his watch, waiting for the hour to strike before he depressed the button of the doorbell.

"Good morning, Cal."

"Fair morning," I replied, thinking of Mary Hartman curled under her kitchen sink, and wondering if there was enough room for me under my own.

Duguay was looking especially fresh and youthful. Dewy.

No, he was wet.

"Your neighbor's sprinkler," he said, shaking out his curls as he stepped inside. "Little wonder everything in his yard looks dead. Your driveway is getting most of the water."

"It works out. He likes his frontage to look like a desert, and I like a clean drive. Unfortunately, he's moving this week. I suppose this is his farewell spray."

"Shouldn't there be music playing?" Duguay asked as we walked to the kitchen and he made his way to his accustomed spot in the breakfast nook. "Like the fountain at the Bellagio."

"I never pegged you as the Vegas type," I said, pouring coffee. I cut a slice of the coconut cake Joshua had left me as a parting gift.

"Thanks. I *love* coconut," Duguay said, reaching out to take the slice of cake. "Joshua?"

"Is my lack of domestic skills that obvious?"

"A simple deduction, Watson."

Clearly, Duguay had inherited some of his parents' acting ability.

"On the occasion of my first visit," he continued, "you offered me Bauli pandoro—a store-bought confection. You have also articulated, on more than one occasion, your ignorance of the culinary arts. Therefore, since it is highly improbable that you could have produced the cake yourself, it was clear to me that the cake must have been the work of your recent houseguest, Summerly, whose reputation as a chef and gourmand aspires to the height of his fame as a bel canto baritone."

"Holmes, you astound me!"

"A simple matter of observation and deduction."

I smiled at the discovery of another shared affinity while I sipped my coffee and Duguay proceeded to devour his cake.

"I'm not, by the way," said Duguay in his normal voice, after he had politely wiped his mouth and folded his napkin into a neat triangle.

"Not what?"

"Not a Vegas type. I went once, with an ex. His mother and father, it turned out, were gamblers. It was planned as a meet-the-parents trip."

"And?"

"I saw the fountain at the Bellagio, and the Red Rocks. Those were the highlights. I never met the parents. Thank God."

"Why 'thank God?'"

"I was way too young for a relationship. And he was too desperate for one. If I'd met mater and pater, and they'd turned out to be nice folks, it would have been easy to get into something it would have been just as difficult to get out of. They probably did me a favor by ignoring me."

"Probably?"

"You never can be sure of your decisions, can you? You can't undo them, of course. But now and then, even years later, you still think about the choices you've made."

Duguay's hand covered mine.

"Even Watson could tell you've been through a rough night," he said softly. "Am I wrong in assuming that is has to do with your memory?"

"Yes," I replied. "I mean no. Sort of. Eric came to see me yesterday and...well...he talked to me about us. About our 'entanglement.' I'd been planning to talk to him, to tell him that it had to end. But he beat me to the punch. It was already ended, apparently."

As I divulged to Duguay the details of my latest encounter with Eric, I felt even more like an asshole than I had the day before.

"And," I concluded, "to top it all off, I've made Eric the fall guy. I hurt his feelings, and it was totally unnecessary and selfish."

"When I was six years old," said Duguay, removing his hand and leaning back against the settle, "I wanted Ernie and Bert hand puppets. I pestered my parents incessantly, but they told me there were no such things. They didn't make them anymore. It was meant to be a tease, you see, on their part. A build-up to the big unveiling on Christmas Eve. But I took them at their word. So, by the time Christmas rolled around, I couldn't have cared less about Ernie and Bert. I remember tearing into that big, shiny package with such anticipation, wondering what in the world was inside. I remember the love—that special 'Christmas feeling'—inside me. And I remember the anger, the utter disappointment when I saw those two silly rubber faces staring up at me. Even though my parents never said anything, I knew they understood how disappointed I was, and I knew I'd hurt their feelings."

I poured more coffee while I digested Duguay's parable.

"So, the moral of the story is 'be careful what you wish for'?" I asked.

"No. My point is that feelings change, desires change. And we can't expect the people we care about to always understand those changes any better than we do ourselves. You're angry with Eric. You're disappointed with yourself. But what's done is done. Accept it and learn from it."

"Why didn't you just *say* that?"

"I just did. May I have another piece of cake?"

I obliged, envying Duguay his youthful disregard of calories and fat.

"If you're not careful," I said, "you'll end up looking like Joshua one of these days."

"Is that such a bad thing? He's a very handsome man."

Pow! A direct hit to my ego.

Duguay examined his cake for a moment, then looked up at me, a twinkle in his eye.

"But he's not my type."

Foolish as it might have been, a wave of relief passed over me—along with a blush, which was hopefully hidden by my copper-brown skin.

"Fish and chips," he added, cleaning the tines of his fork with his mouth. "We still have a date, right?"

A *date*?

"Of course. Whenever is good for you."

"How about today? Yoga, our usual power walk, then one more trip to the beach? No skinny-dipping; I promise."

*

Sitting at a wooden table in the picnic area, fully exposed to the sun in a cloudless sky, Duguay and I enjoyed the cool breeze off the Sound as we partook of our battered codfish, thick-cut fried potatoes, and homemade cream soda.

"Many thanks for the beachside feast."

Duguay raised his glass of soda. "It makes me wish we were in China."

"Come again?"

"You know. They say the Chinese consider burping during a meal to be good table manners."

"I did warn you about that second piece of cake."

Not wanting our fry-ups to get cold, we continued to eat in silence.

When we'd both pushed away our empty plates, I said, "Thanks for the advice this morning."

"It was included in the package," he replied. "My last official act of commiseration."

"So, this is it?"

"You've made excellent progress in your physical recuperation, and your memory impairment does not appear to have any detrimental effect on your day-to-day life. You don't exhibit any signs of post-traumatic psychosis." Duguay shrugged. "I can't justify a request for an extension of my services."

I noted hesitation in Duguay's voice.

"You'd like to keep me, but you have to let me go?" I asked.

Duguay raised an eyebrow.

"Something Malhotra said to me when I checked out of the funny farm."

"Oh."

Duguay toyed with his apparently empty fish and chip basket, discovered a hidden fragment of a chip and ate it.

"I really like you, Cal," he said, wiping his fingers with a napkin. "I've come to think of you as more of a friend than a patient. And I'd like to get to know you better. But I'm not sure if now is the right time. You've still got a lot you need to work through...on your own."

I feared broadcasting my disappointment through my facial expression, so I attempted a pensive look and rubbed my chin. After all, it wasn't exactly a brushoff—though I wouldn't have blamed Duguay if it had been. He had a point. Recently adulterous, recently separated, recently widowed, and currently semi-amnesiac, I was hardly a prize package. I nodded acceptance.

"Getting back to teaching will help," added Duguay. "It'll give you focus—provide an outlet for reconnecting to the wider world while still giving you enough 'me' time."

"Funny you should mention work," I said. "Declan, Melody, Jill, and Eric—"

"Sounds like that Mazursky film."

"Huh?"

Duguay made a forget-about-it gesture. "We won't always be able to understand each other's references."

I smiled at the hopeful tense of Duguay's reply.

"Anyway," I continued, "they don't seem too enthusiastic about my return. Joshua's opinion is that they're either concerned for my health or afraid I'll lose it and cause some sort of drama at the center."

Duguay shook his head. "I can't see that happening. But your friends don't have my professional insight. They understand that you're still, to some degree, emotionally fragile. And that makes them nervous."

"So, you're saying I should cut them some slack and let them think I could possibly be a nutjob?"

"No. Look, if you like, I can have an unofficial word with Melody...let her know I've given you the all clear."

"You'd do that?"

"Of course. She's the center's volunteer coordinator, right? So, then she'll receive official notice from Dr. Malhotra. But a personal touch never hurts."

"Thank you."

"*De nada.* We can swing by the center on the way back to your place."

"Perfect."

I was looking forward to introducing Melody to Duguay, and I was anxious to be at the center again, to reconnect to something good from my life.

Duguay looked down at the table and toyed with his empty fish basket.

"I also have a selfish reason for wanting you to get back into your volunteer work," he added.

"Really? What?"

"Well, I figure if you start teaching again, you'll start painting again." He looked up at me and smiled. "And when you start painting again, I'll know the time is right."

I didn't ask what for. I took Duguay's smile as the answer.

It was as we stood up to take our leave that the memory hit me. Was it Duguay's mention of painting? Was it something in the way he smiled that reminded me of a youthful Paul? I can't say for sure, but events from ten years before seemed suddenly immediate, and the recollection filled me with sadness and conflicted emotions. I didn't realize I was crying until Duguay handed me a napkin.

"Hey, what's wrong?" he asked.

"A memory. Out of nowhere." I wiped my eyes with the course paper. "I hate this shit," I added, looking away toward the Sound.

"Cheap napkins or sudden memory flashes?"

"Both," I replied, laughing, relieved.

"Do you want to tell me about it?"

I nodded, still looking out toward the water.

"Walk with me?"

I headed to the beach, and Duguay followed.

"Our first vacation together," I began as the surf licked our bare feet. "Paul and me." Duguay waited patiently while I gathered my thoughts. "Just into our second year as a couple. We'd planned on Machu Picchu—someplace neither of us had been. But Paul pulled a rabbit out of the hat at the last minute; he booked a trip to Paris instead. I loved Paris—I still do—but I'd really been looking forward to Peru. Paris was nothing new for either of us."

"You were angry with Paul?"

"Yeah. At first. But when he explained to me why he'd done it, I felt...I felt special. I loved him so much at that moment. He told me he wanted to see Paris with me—through my eyes. I used to tell Paul about my time there as an art student. He wanted to see my old apartment building, the school, my favorite art supply store on the Quai Voltaire. Everything that had made it beautiful for me. Everything I'd loved, Paul wanted to know."

I kicked at the wet sand and turned to face Duguay.

"It was wonderful, Marc. And you know what? I forgot all about it until today. Even after I saved the mug from the trash bin. I understood its significance, but the emotions were...buried. Until now."

"A mug?"

"Yes. It was our last night. Paul had planned a romantic dinner at some ludicrously expensive, Michelin-starred restaurant—but I came down with a cold. It was raining, and I was miserable, so Paul brought the feast to us. Four courses served and consumed in bed. I don't remember what the food tasted like, really. I was too congested. But it didn't matter."

I started to choke up and took a calming breath.

"The last course was followed by champagne and a gift. I looked at this box wrapped in exquisite foil paper and tied with an organza ribbon and thought, Oh, my God, it's a ring. Or a watch, or a bracelet. You know, a serious 'relationship' gift. But when I opened it, I was so disappointed. I guess I felt like you must have done with the Ernie and Bert puppets."

"It was the mug?"

"Yeah. With crude renderings of the Eiffel tower, the Arc de Triomphe, and the windmills of Montmartre on one side. The other side of the cup was emblazoned with 'We'll Always Have Paris' and two hearts. It was a very romantic gesture, but I didn't appreciate it at the time."

"And now?"

"I don't know. I don't think our love survived past those first few years. We became a habit. Something easy and familiar. We never made love again the way we did that night—hungry for each other, almost desperate. They say familiarity breeds contempt. It must be true. Paul and

I did nothing but argue toward the end. Either we weren't the same people anymore, or we'd never taken a good look at ourselves or each other. I don't know how I would have felt when Paul died if I'd still been in love with him. As it was, what I felt was relief. I know that sounds horrible... but... It's hard to explain."

"I think you're doing a pretty good job."

"Thanks. I feel sad that Paul's gone...sad for everything that was and no longer is. Yet, at the same time, I'm happy. Happy to be free. Happy to have been saved from what could have been years of misery—never being able to let go and move on. Sometimes, I feel like I want to cry and dance at the same time."

"So, why don't you?"

"It's that simple?"

Duguay shrugged. "There's no one-size-fits-all solution to the processing of grief and the acceptance of loss. No two relationships are the same, therefore, no one's mourning for a partner, a friend, or a family member can be the same."

"I understand what you're saying. But how can I get past the fact that the last words I said to him were angry words?"

"You can't Cal. You can't undo those last moments, that final argument. But you know what?"

"What?"

Duguay put a hand on my shoulder and squeezed.

"You *still* have Paris."

Chapter Eight

MARC

Invoking the axiom of striking while the iron is hot, I suggested we stop by the Hollyford Community Center on our way back to Cal's house. He seemed surprised, but he agreed. I guessed Cal assumed I'd planned on calling on Ms. Lewis alone. During the short drive from the beach to the center, I explained to Cal that his company would help to ensure that the visit was interpreted as strictly casual, even spur of the moment—which, indeed, it was. However, my principal motivation came from the desire to observe Cal's social interaction.

I had spent some time in the company of Cal and his friend, Joshua, but theirs was almost a familial relationship. I needed an outside perspective. What I wanted, really, was to reassure myself that my evaluation of Cal's condition was accurate. A test drive. Despite what I'd said to Cal, and what I'd already written in my report to Dr. Malhotra, I couldn't shake the feeling I was missing something.

Most people understand the importance of trust in a practitioner-patient relationship, but many only consider the trust a patient puts in the practitioner, not the other way around. Despite my growing affection for Cal, I had yet to feel that I trusted him. Although we all lie sometimes, there were different kinds of liars. There were those who lied effortlessly, others who struggled with even the most innocent falsehood. I suspected Cal was one of the former. Nevertheless, what Cal was lying about and whether he was lying to himself or to me (or both) remained a mystery. I hoped I would find some clues at the center.

At a distance, I thought Melody Lewis was what my mother would call "a full-figured gal." She certainly did not exhibit any signs of shame relating to her proportions. Indeed, she flaunted her form in a low-cut, sleeveless shift of the most dazzling electric-blue stretch material. Around her slim neck, she wore a lapis and silver necklace of Native American design. The smile on her pretty and expertly made-up face was genuine and welcoming.

"The Delectable Duguay, at last!" she cried as she squeezed me in greeting. I shot a look at Cal, who shrugged and mouthed *Joshua*. I decided to play along.

"The Lovely Ms. Lewis, at last!"

Melody laughed as she stepped back from her hug.

"So far, so good. Let me see your left hand." I obliged. "No wedding band. Cha-ching!"

"I'm gay."

"Damn. Oh well, nothing wrong with eye candy. Come on, then. Let me show you the place."

Cal followed silently in our wake as Melody gave me the grand tour of the Hollyford Community Center.

"The sign on my desk says Volunteer Coordinator," declared Melody as she sashayed through the modest facility. "But I'm chief cook and bottle washer, now that Hyacinth has retired."

"Wallace Norwood," interjected Cal, coming up to my side. "Hollyford's male version of Hyacinth Bucket."

"And an excellent administrator," said Melody. "Replacing him will be a challenge."

We entered a large, glass-ceilinged room filled with easels, stools, and myriad art paraphernalia. Like many of the commercial enterprises in the older part of Hollyford, the center occupied a repurposed antique property. The art room had originally been the solarium of a Victorian-era home and, filled as it was with natural light, served its new role well.

Cal proceeded to make a circuit of the room, looking at, touching, adjusting, and shifting objects here and there. Melody and I stood aside, silent, both appreciating the importance of this moment for Cal.

"Everything's just as you left it," said Melody eventually as Cal turned to face us with a small smile on his lips. "I put it to a vote. None of your students wanted to continue with a different instructor—not as long as there was a good chance of you returning. They were loyal to a one."

Melody's voice quavered with her last words. My opinion of Melody bumped up a notch as I realized there was much more to her than superficial charm, and that her affection for Cal ran deeper than that of professional courtesy.

Although Cal's smile remained intact, he appeared on the brink of tears, and his hand trembled slightly atop his wolf-head walking stick.

"I—" Cal gulped and took a deep breath. "Could you guys give me a minute?"

"Sure, honey," said Melody. "I'll fix us all a cup of coffee. Meet us in my office when you're ready."

No sooner had we entered Melody's diminutive domain than she gripped me by the forearm. "I need your help, Delectable Duguay."

The urgency and sincerity in her voice were clear, despite the flippancy of her delivery.

"At your service," I replied.

"Thank you." She looked over my shoulder in the direction of the room where we'd left Cal, then back at me. "It's about Cal."

Here it comes.

I steeled myself and put on my best caring-medical-practitioner face.

Melody waved a dismissive hand as she turned toward the cubby that housed her espresso machine.

"I don't want to talk to you as a professional," she said, sticking a pod in the machine. "I want to talk to you as a friend of Cal's."

"Melody, I'm not really—"

Melody laughed. "Oh, cut the bull. I know the 'look' when I see it."

"The 'look'?"

"Um-hum. Puppy dog eyes. You've got it bad, doc."

"Nurse practitioner," I corrected, not bothering to deny the veracity of the rest of Melody's words. "How can I help you?"

Melody's expression turned serious. "I don't have time to go into details now. Can I give you a call later today?"

"Of course."

I pulled a card from my wallet and handed it to Melody, intrigued but uneasy. I felt as if I were doing something behind Cal's back. Probably because I was.

When Cal joined us, he found Melody and me discussing the virtues of pod coffee makers.

"I feel like Norma Desmond returning to Paramount," said Cal, accepting an espresso from Melody.

And he looked it too. Radiant, triumphant. I just hoped his comeback would be more successful than that of the fictitious delusional film star.

"I passed by Laura's Pilates class," continued Cal, "and everyone came out to greet me."

"Your adoring public," said Melody, smiling. "It's been like a morgue here without you."

Then, Melody's smile disappeared, and I could practically feel her wince at her verbal fumble.

"Oh God, Cal, I'm so sorry," she said as I watched the animation fade from Cal's face. "I know I can be tactless sometimes, but that was unforgivable."

"It's all right," replied Cal. "You don't have to walk on eggshells. I'm coming back to work to get on with my life, not dwell on the past. Which brings me to why I've brought Marc with me today." Cal lifted his cup to me and gave a small bow. "Go ahead; tell the nice lady that I'm fit for duty."

"My patient speaks the truth," I said to Melody. "He's good to go."

The smile returned to Melody's face, and I had to wonder, since she was apparently more than happy to welcome Cal back into the fold, what the heck she needed to speak with me privately about.

Once we'd refilled our coffees and talked about the center for a few minutes, Melody indicated she needed to get back to work. Cal and I said goodbye to our host and returned to Cal's home.

Pulling out of Cal's driveway a few minutes later, I experienced a powerful sense of regret as I watched him wave goodbye, Bruno obediently at his side.

I'd never fallen in love with a patient before. But, as they say, there is a first time for everything.

My little house welcomed me with the comforts of one's own domain, and I felt much less depressed and conflicted as I relaxed on my old velvet sofa and enjoyed a rare moment of solitude with a bottle of brown ale in one hand and *Northanger Abby* in the other.

Then my phone rang.

"Marc? It's Melody Lewis."

"Hi, Melody. Thanks again for the tour and the coffee. So, what's up?"

I listened to a deep intake of breath and a long sigh.

"It's one of Cal's students," said Melody. I heard the creak of an office chair followed by a huff. "William Blake. He committed suicide two weeks after Cal's accident." Melody paused, made a tsk sound. "He doesn't know, Marc. Cal doesn't know. We don't know how to tell him—

not on top of everything else. As if Paul's death wasn't enough. I know their relationship was on the rocks—and I'm not breaking a confidence by telling you so—but the circumstances...the accident... I can't even begin to imagine how Cal must feel."

No, you can't. The guilt, the responsibility Cal feels will never be completely erased. How he deals with this will shape the man he will be for the rest of his life...

I didn't say this to Melody. Nor did I tell her I hoped to be part of that life. Instead, I returned to the subject of William Blake.

"Were they close?" I asked. "Cal and William Blake?"

Close could mean anything, and I steeled myself for Melody's answer.

"No." She stretched out the word in a way that seemed to negate it's meaning. "William admired Cal, and Cal considered William his best student. I'd have to agree with Cal on that. William is—*was* brilliant. He and Cal had a solid mentor-pupil relationship, but I wouldn't say they were close as *friends*, if you know what I mean. Cal makes a strict point of not encouraging familiarity with his students—he even insists they address him as Mr. Restrepo, though the environment at the center is far from formal."

"Well, then, I can certainly see Cal will be upset by the news, but I don't imagine it will deter him from continuing his work...if that's what you're worried about."

There was something else; I could feel it. But I also got the feeling that whatever it was, Melody wasn't going to share it. At least, not yet.

"So, I can assume Cal never mentioned William to you?" Melody continued. "I realize it's inappropriate for me to ask you—and for you to answer—but, well, if Cal doesn't remember William, it puts a different spin on things, doesn't it? We'd have to approach things in an entirely different way."

"I see," I replied, impressed with the subtlety of Melody's thinking. "Unfortunately, Cal has never spoken to me of William Blake, so your guess is as good as mine as to whether or not he remembers him. I have to say this looks like a clear case of honesty being the best policy. And the sooner you tell Cal, the better."

"That's what I think too. Declan's talked me into hedging, but it goes against my instincts."

A thought occurred to me, prompted by what Cal had related to me of his conversation with Joshua about his return to work.

"Does Joshua Summerly know about William's suicide?"

There was a slight pause before Melody replied. A guilty pause, I imagined.

"No. We thought that might complicate matters further."

"We," meaning Declan, no doubt. The priest probably thought he was doing the right thing, but he, of all people, should have understood that the road to hell is paved with good intentions.

"Cal and Joshua appear to have a very strong bond," I said. "I should think Joshua would be the best person to break the news to Cal. Keeping him out of the loop might not have been the best idea."

Another pause followed by a small huff.

Melody did not need to tell me that this, too, had been Declan's idea. Declan, the meddlesome priest.

"It's not too late, Melody."

"Joshua's in Tuscany until the end of August."

Shit.

"Look, Melody. You called me because you wanted my advice, right? Well, my advice is to tell Cal ASAP. Don't pull punches. Forget about Declan. Follow your heart and do what you think is right."

"That last part sounds like a line from a movie."

"It probably is. But it works here, I think."

Melody thanked me and said goodbye, promising to keep me posted.

On the one hand, I felt like the King of the Wusses for not volunteering to be the bearer of bad news—which I was convinced was why Melody had reached out to me. On the other hand, I told myself I'd done the right thing. I'd already behaved unprofessionally with Cal. I'd crossed lines, however subtly and however well-intentioned. I didn't need to compound this by interfering in Cal's personal life: to do so would ring the death nell on any possible future relationship with him.

Having lost interest in the adventures of Catherine Morland, I marked my page and closed the book, then finished off my ale and opened another bottle. I thought about dinner and settled on nachos. As I spread the tortilla chips on a baking sheet, grated cheese, and sliced jalapenos, I recalled Cal's warning. He was right, of course. At thirty-six, I was nearing the end of the high-metabolism phase of my life. My boyish figure could turn to a dad bod overnight if I wasn't careful.

I blamed my poor eating habits on my work. Between my evening shift on the volunteer roster at a local hospital and my "day" job as a visiting practitioner, there wasn't much time for any extracurricular activity other than sleep. But this was my choice; to complain would be to admit to an error in judgement. I wanted to be busy. I needed it. To have time on my hands would lead to boredom. Boredom would lead to loneliness...

As I waited for the nachos to bubble and brown, I allowed myself a moment of reflection on my solitary state. Lately, I found these moments occurring more and more, and this bothered me. Following the end of a short, intense but ultimately untenable relationship, I'd vowed to spend the rest of my life single, immune to disappointment, to infidelity. Over the last ten years, I'd built my fortress—my life dedicated to strangers and my retreat in my little Cape Cod with its fireplace and collection of classic literature—and the walls had held fast.

Until Calixto Restrepo limped into my life.

Chapter Nine

CAL

Finally, memories began to return in waves rather than in flashes—whole blocks of time, years of experiences were suddenly just *there*, part of my consciousness. Both Dr. Malhotra and Joshua had spoken of triggers—people, places, or things that could unlock the doors in my mind. Bruno had been one such trigger. The center had been another.

Standing there in the art room, I'd felt truly whole again in the space of a few moments. Well, not truly, *completely* whole, but as close as I'd been to such a state since I'd left Wending Hills. It was close to a sensory overload: The smells, the light, the textures. The *sounds*. Yes, the sounds. I recalled the sounds of my students' voices, the sounds of easels scraping against the wood floor, turned, repositioned, stools adjusted. The sound of a model's sigh of exasperation as I cajoled him or her into holding a pose for just a few moments longer.

I'd encouraged my students to take turns modeling, to put themselves on the other side of the easel. I often found that those—like William Blake—who excelled as artists were also excellent subjects of artistic study.

I realized that I missed William. Missed all my students.

Suddenly, I felt a sense of time wasted. I'd been living in a prison in my mind, standing still while the world marched on outside. The visit to the center had been an awakening. It was time for me to get my ass in gear.

Thank you, Duguay.

And Melody.

They'd hit it off. What a relief *that* was. There aren't many things worse than being in a relationship with someone who none of your friends like. I'd been there and done that. If something special did develop between Duguay and me, I wanted to share it with everyone, not keep it locked away like a plant without air, sunshine, and water until it withered and died.

I poured a glass of white wine and took it out to the backyard, where I could enjoy both it and the soft, fading evening light. Lazing on the swing, I gazed at the pinkish-purple sky and the tufts of clouds and my thoughts returned to William. Words we'd exchanged during a break in class came into my mind and brought a smile to my face.

"Hey, Mr. Restrepo."

"Hey, William. What's up?"

"I finally get it!"

"Get what?"

"What you were saying about light. How you can't make it up."

"I did?"

"Yeah. Remember? I kept insisting that I could paint just as well from a picture—or from memory—and you said: 'No. Light can never be reproduced secondhand. You need to capture it when you see it. Memories play tricks on you and photographs lie.' Man, you were so right! I was sitting on the beach, you know, watching the sunrise. The light was incredible. That's when I understood. I felt it. I knew at that moment that color was only then and never again. You can't invent a sunrise; you just paint the sunrise you see."

I wondered how William was faring. It was late July. He might have moved to New York already if he'd found a place off campus. Not likely, considering his parents' financial situation. Now that I was beginning to think clearly and have a more normal sense of time passing, I remembered that two of my older students would also be moving away to further their artistic education in the fall, one to Rhode Island and another to Florence. I'd always kept a rather formal distance from my students, but I vowed to loosen up a bit in the future. I would begin by checking up on them and thanking them for their good wishes while I was hospitalized.

And I would start with William.

I returned to the house. After refreshing my wine, I went to my workroom and opened my laptop. Never having bothered with a password, I was online quickly and soon logged in to the staff/faculty page of the center. According to center policy, I had access to student email addresses, but not physical addresses or telephone numbers. William was an exception. As the only minor enrolled in my classes, his parents' full contact information was listed in lieu of his own.

I picked up my cell and dialed the Blakes' number, feeling guilty that I'd never called to congratulate them on William's success.

An answer after three rings.

"Mrs. Blake? Hello, this is Cal Restrepo. I'm sorry if—"

Click.

I redialed.

No answer.

I hung up, trying to ignore the queasy, intuitive feeling of wrongness that came over me.

I suddenly remembered the day my mother died—or, more precisely, the day after. I'd come home late, following a successful Broadway premier and a boozy after party, but not too late for my mom in California. She'd want to know all the details. The phone rang and rang. No answer. No machine. I yawned, shrugged, and went to sleep. In the afternoon, I woke and called again. No answer. Her housekeeper, Nilda, called me three hours later.

She'd found my mother on the sofa, a book in her lap, bent over as if she'd fallen asleep. Nilda told me that a porcelain cup lay shattered on the immaculate parquet floor in a small pool of chocolate. Her favorite after dinner reading accompaniment.

She'd been dead for quite some time, according to the paramedics.

She'd died from a stroke while I drank champagne.

The grief and the guilt welled up anew.

Why now?

Why am I remembering this now?

Why had Mrs. Blake hung up on me...ignored my call?

I took a deep breath, steadied myself, took a gulp of wine.

Be rational. Why would Mrs. Blake hang up on you? The Blakes probably moved, changed their number. Lots of folks move when their kids graduate from high school.

Yet, I was certain it was Rhea Blake's voice I'd heard.

I couldn't shake the sense of foreboding. After all, there were many things I still couldn't remember...

I nearly called Joshua but was too frazzled to calculate the time change. Then, I thought of Marc.

I swiped open my phone.

Would I look desperate? Needy? Weak?

Why not? That was how I felt.

It's been less than a week. Give the man space.

I called Declan instead.

*

Declan sat in what I now thought of as Duguay's spot. It had never been Paul's spot. Paul disliked eating in the kitchen, and his legs were too long to fit comfortably in the nook. Though Declan was nearly as tall, the distance from his hips to his knees was clearly shorter than Paul's had been, allowing Declan to sit quite comfortably with one leg crossed over the other.

"How are you settling into your new digs?" I asked, as I poured red wine.

"Quite nicely, thank you. The place has been recently treated to what I believe is called a gut reno. A twee rectory on the outside, a sleek bachelor pad on the inside. Very comfortable. I've even inherited my predecessor's housekeeper—though I've yet to decide if that's a good thing."

I smiled, and we drank in silence for a few minutes.

"So," said Declan, setting his glass on the table, "what troubles you, Cal?"

Declan's voice was a just a fraction lower than normal. His confessional voice, I supposed.

"Practicing?" I asked.

"I beg your pardon?"

"Sorry. I just couldn't help picturing a little screen between us."

Declan laughed and swirled his wine.

"How was I?"

"Not bad."

"All right, then. Shoot."

"It's about William," I said.

Declan's gaze shifted to his glass.

"I called his mother earlier and...well, she hung up on me. At least, I think she did. I mean, have they moved? Do I have the wrong number?"

"No, Cal. The Blakes haven't moved or changed their number as far as I know."

"So, what's wrong? Did the Blakes and I have a falling out of some kind? Did William and I get into an argument we left unresolved?" I looked out the window into the garden, then turned back to Declan. "Or—or has something happened to William?"

I saw the answer in Declan's eyes. My premonition validated.

"No," I whispered as Declan reached out to touch my hand. "No."

"I'm sorry, Cal. William passed away shortly after your accident."

"He just turned eighteen!"

Declan didn't flinch at my anguished outburst, merely gripped my hand tighter. I bent my head over the top of Declan's hand, feeling sucker punched.

"I'm so sorry, Cal," he repeated. "Sorry for William...and sorry that I didn't tell you sooner. I—we—we didn't know how to break it to you. Didn't even know if you remembered William. We were waiting for the right time...not knowing if there ever would be a right time."

I pulled away from Declan and wiped a tear from my eye.

"How?"

Declan pulled at his hair and sighed.

"How did he die, Declan?"

"William took his own life."

"Jesus Christ."

I looked out to the garden again, trying to ground myself in something good, something right.

"Why? He was...strange in some ways; introverted, yeah. But suicidal? I can't believe it. What could possibly—" I stopped short, remembering my call to Mrs. Blake. I turned back to Declan. "Was it something I said? Something I did? Oh, God. I couldn't live with myself if..." I pushed my hands against my face in frustration.

"It wasn't you. The Blakes don't blame you directly. They're just mad at the world right now."

"Then, what? Drugs? No way. Not William."

"No, there was no question of substance abuse. William was distraught. Depressed. Mr. and Mrs. Blake sought me out for counseling. They made appointments with a psychiatrist. William refused to go. He withdrew. He even talked of giving up on art school, on his future."

"That makes no sense. It was all he dreamed of."

Declan shook his head. "I don't know. I couldn't reach him. All he would say to me was that if God existed, God was evil because he made the innocent suffer. He was so full of anger, so different from the gentle, optimistic lad I'd believed him to be."

"Believed him to be?"

"There are some people who are the same on the outside as on the inside, but they are rare—one counts oneself lucky to have such people in one's life. They make friendships and intimate relationships easy. People like your friend, Joshua. For all his camp and drama, one gets the sense that he's *true*. Wouldn't you agree? Perhaps it's because he's an actor. He lives out fantasies, other lives on the stage—he has no need to pretend in real life. The rest of us...we wear masks in our daily lives. We change those masks to fit in, to be accepted, to be loved. Most of us are chameleons. It's how we survive."

"Or not."

"Indeed. I can only assume that William, though so young, was skilled at hiding his inner self...that something critical must have occurred to cause the curtain to be raised, the mask to be removed."

I mulled over Declan's theory and had to agree. What I had considered ethereal, quirky, and charming in William's personality and behavior could have been the signs of inner turmoil held under tenuous wraps. I only knew the William that he chose to show me. If only I'd looked deeper. If only...

"I failed him, Declan."

"We all feel we fail one another at times. I could have, I would have, I should have. At the end of the day, we do what we do. If we strive to do our best, there is nothing more to be done. You gave William 110 percent as a teacher and artistic mentor. Don't beat yourself up because you couldn't be his father, mother, brother, or best friend."

"I know. Intellectually, I know you're right. Emotionally, well..." I thought of Declan's mother; her illness and death. Of Declan's devotion up until the end. "You understand."

Declan nodded. Silence drew out as he finished his wine with uncharacteristic speed. When I'd refilled his glass, Declan said:

"Do you remember me telling you how my mother's death was a release?"

"Yes."

"Well, though it goes against my faith to condone suicide, the only way I can understand it, accept it, is to consider it a release from suffering. And I believe that God will also understand. We may not know what drove William to take his own life, but we have to accept that, for him, the alternative was worse."

Declan reached out his free hand across the table, palm up.

"Will you pray with me, Cal?"

I stared at Declan for a moment, then lowered my head and reached out to take his hand.

"Dear Heavenly Father, we pray for the soul of William. We ask that, in your infinite kindness and mercy, you welcome him into your kingdom of light and love, that he will find eternal peace in your dwelling place. Father, we pray also for the soul of Paul. May he find the joy in your presence which he sought in devotion to you here on Earth."

I looked up at Declan and whispered, "And for Elspeth too."

Declan smiled, then continued. "Lastly, Father, we pray for ourselves. May we be forgiven our sins; may we forgive those who sin against us." Declan squeezed my hand a litter tighter. "And, Father, may we be given the grace to forgive ourselves and trust in the guidance of your divine presence. Amen."

"Amen."

Declan let go of my hand, and I wiped my eyes with the back of it.

"Thank you, Declan."

*

Several weeks later, I received a call from Rhea Blake, inviting me to meet her and her husband for wine and canapes. Though I suspected it had been Declan's machinations that had brought about this social call, I accepted without hesitation. I like the Blakes, and I was eager to mend whatever tear had been rent in our previously friendly relationship.

From without, the home of Edward and Rhea Blake appeared to be an unremarkable, if classic, California raised ranch. Within, it looked as if brutal renovations had stripped away all wood and carpeting and had transformed what must have been an already open floor plan into a loftlike space with a decidedly industrial vibe. Where once beams had probably existed, HVAC ducts hung suspended along with enormous, globe-shaped crystal pendant lights. The cantilevered stairway leading to the second floor was a showpiece of steel and glass. Sleek sofas and chairs were cleverly arranged atop the expanse of poured concrete floor to draw the eye inward and beyond to the wall of glass that offered a view of sloping green lawn and lakefront.

"Wow," I said, taking it all in as Rhea Blake ushered me into her living room, where we sat down.

"I wish I could take credit for it," said Mrs. Blake. "But it came this way."

"Really? I assumed it was an ambitious reno."

"No. It was a model for a development that went bust. Edward and I bought it at auction."

Mrs. Blake looked around the room with something of a wistful expression, and her smile faded. "Billy hated it."

Rhea Blake hugged herself, curling inward. Then, she sighed and sat straight, shaking her head of loose blond curls. She was an attractive, athletically built woman in her late thirties, but grief had aged her cruelly. The large blue eyes that had once sparkled were now dull, dark circles and puffiness underscoring their unfocused look, and her mouth was set in a tight line.

"I apologize again for my behavior on the phone that day," Mrs. Blake continued. "My rudeness was uncalled for."

"Please, Mrs. Blake—"

"Rhea."

"Please, Rhea. You don't need to apologize. I can't pretend to understand what you feel right now, but I do know something about what you're going through."

Rhea nodded. "Which makes my rudeness even more unforgivable. You were calling me to offer your condolences... Even with all *you've* been through, you made the effort to reach out."

I didn't contradict her. Had I known of William's death at the time of the call, that certainly would have been my intention.

"Thank you for inviting me here and allowing me to do so in person," I replied.

"I'm glad you came. Billy never stopped talking about you. He admired you. Looked up to you."

Rhea paused, and a slight narrowing of her eyes led me to believe she was considering adding something.

Whatever it might have been was interrupted by the sound of a key turning in the front door and the security system being disabled.

"Edward," said Rhea, rising.

The husky, red-haired man strode into the room and wrapped his wife in a tight, unselfconscious hug.

"Ed," continued Mrs. Blake, pulling with obvious reluctance from the embrace, "you remember Cal Restrepo?"

"Of course."

I accepted Edward Blake's hand, feeling the roughness of its skin and the strength of its grip. It was a comfortable, warm hand and I thought that those two adjectives could equally describe the owner of that hand. I recalled meeting him for the first time at the center and immediately thinking, *What a nice man*. Nice. The word is so often used in an almost pejorative, condescending way. But in its proper, positive sense, "nice" suited Edward Blake down to the ground.

We exchanged the awkward, perfunctory condolences of the recently bereaved and then settled in front of the fireplace while Mrs. Blake retrieved a bottle of Riesling and three glasses from the large, open kitchen.

"Delicious," I lied, having taken a sip of my least favorite variety of wine. Grateful, however, that it wasn't tea or coffee, I think I managed to sound sincere.

For a few uncomfortable moments, we three drank our wine and partook of Mrs. Blake's dainty, homemade pastries.

Then Edward Blake said, "Look, Cal, we didn't invite you here to sit around and feel sorry for ourselves.

As hard as it is for Rhea and me, we've come to the point when we know it's time to move on, get on with our lives as best we can." He reached an arm around his wife's shoulder and pulled her close. "We've decided to honor the traditions of our Irish ancestors and celebrate Billy's life rather than mourn the lack of it."

Rhea Blake wiped a tear away, took a drink of wine.

"That's why we wanted to see you," she added. "We need your help."

My help?

"This is the thing," said Blake, leaning forward and resting his elbows on his muscular thighs. "Billy left a bunch of paintings...his work, his portfolio. We thought, well, what are we going to do with it? Make a shrine of his room?" Blake shook his head. "We don't want to go down that road. What we've decided is that we want to share it. Exhibit it. So everyone can know how talented Billy was...see the goodness that was in him."

Blake choked up, bent down and pressed a fist to his mouth. His wife gently caressed his shoulders.

"We don't know anything about art," said Rhea, picking up her husband's thread. "We have no idea where to begin. We just know what we want to do, and we hoped you could guide us. Be Billy's *curator*. If that's the right word."

William's father raised his head and nodded his agreement.

As I looked from one loving, devasted parent to the other, I found it difficult to hold back my own tears and it took an effort to bring the words of my response down from my brain into my mouth and out.

"I would be honored."

*

Edward Blake arrived at my house the next day, his car filled with his son's artwork. After transporting the haul to my workroom, Edward accepted my invitation to coffee. We settled on the sunroom as the best place to enjoy our java.

"I told myself I wouldn't talk about Billy," said Edward after we'd sipped in silence for a few moments. "Said to myself there must be a million other things to say. But there's nothing much else on my mind these days."

"I understand," I murmured over the rim of my mug—the Paris mug. As my memories continued their frustratingly slow download, those of Paul were piling up quickly in the "recent files" of my mind.

"You know," I continued, "when I first came back from Wending Hills, I used to wish I'd never recovered some memories—to think that it would have been a blessing to have forgotten Paul and our life together. A clean reboot. Now, I appreciate how important those memories are, how precious—even if they're sad memories. They're part of who I am. William was your son. I can't imagine there will ever be a time when he's not part of you. With you in some way or another. Don't fight the memories, Edward. Let them come."

Edward Blake smiled through the tears that were slowing dripping into his coffee.

"Now I know why Billy thought you were so great." He swiped the back of his free hand against his eyes. "I wish I could have been able to talk to Billy like you did."

What?

"We never talked about anything but art."

"I know. That's what I mean. Art was everything to Billy. If I could have understood it...shared his interest, maybe we could've been close. Maybe..."

Edward shrugged, the significance of the "maybe" clear. My heart went out to him, but I could think of no words of comfort that would not sound empty or condescending.

"My first wife died when Billy was twelve," Edward continued. "Billy wasn't the same after that. Not with me. He was never angry or bratty, nothing like that. He just closed himself off. I worried about remarrying. I didn't want to put Billy though the stereotypical I-hate-my-stepmother phase. But then, I met Rhea. I loved her so much, how could Billy not love her too? You know?

"I never knew how he felt about her, really. He'd say, 'She's great.' Or, 'I'm happy for you, Dad.' Stuff like that. But there was always that distance, the feeling that Billy was with us but somewhere else in his head. With Billy's painting and all, I thought, well, maybe it was what they call 'artistic temperament.' I guess it was easier to believe that than think Billy blamed me for his mother's death and resented Rhea's place in our lives."

Edward shrugged again, clearly a movement that was part of his conversational style, just as hand gestures were to others. He finished off his coffee and placed his empty mug on the floor between our chairs.

"Several months ago, Billy changed. It was like a light went on inside him. It was weird. We'd gotten so used to this quiet, withdrawn kid. At first, we worried it might be drugs. But it was around the time Billy got accepted to Cooper Union. I figured that was what did it—the one thing that really made him happy in the years since his mother died. Rhea had another idea. She said that if she didn't know any better, Billy was in love."

I smiled a little, recalling the excitement, the euphoria of reading my own college acceptance letter. Indeed, it had felt like being in love.

"Rhea pegged Belinda Lindstrom as the likely siren," added Edward. "But I couldn't see it. They'd been friends since grammar school. And, well, I wasn't sure if...if Billy even *liked* girls. I mean, you know."

I did know. What I didn't know—hadn't known or remembered—was that William and Eric's daughter had been friends. Something about this newfound knowledge unsettled me, but I couldn't quite put my finger on it.

"Billy didn't ever, um, confide in you? Man-to-man?"

Edward asked the question bluntly enough, but I could hear the pleading in his words, the wish for an answer he could comprehend to an event that was beyond comprehension.

"I'm sorry, Edward. No. My relationship with William wasn't that close."

"Oh—I—I didn't mean that because you're—I mean. Fuck. I don't know what I'm saying."

"Don't sweat it. I understand. And, truthfully, I did get the sense that William was gay. But, as I said, we never talked about that kind of thing. It was always art."

I paused, groping for words to express my feelings about and understanding of the young man who had only recently found his way back into my memory. "I thought I knew William, though, through his art," I said finally. "Some part of him, at least. And I loved that part of him. It was like seeing myself thirty-five years ago. But, looking back, I realize there was so much I didn't see, didn't know."

Edward nodded slowly. "That's just it. There was so much I didn't know. And now, I'll never know."

Silence returned, and with it, a feeling of sad kinship with Edward Blake. I imagined he felt it, too, as we watched the roses undulate in the breeze.

Chapter Ten

My first day back teaching at the center. The welcome, the genuine goodwill I felt from my students and fellow instructors was fantastic. As my students arrived, I was subjected to embraces, shoulder slaps, and the occasional kiss. Nothing could have prepared me for this outpouring of kindness. Even those students who were new to the class had been apprised of my recent adversity and offered their good wishes.

It was too much.

I cried.

I moved in a joyous dream, critiquing here, cajoling there.

I was home.

God, had it only been a few months?

It felt like a lifetime.

Only toward the end of the class did the dreamscape flicker and flirt with a nightmare vision: I looked upon the innocuous arrangement of fruits and vegetables on the central platform and saw the naked body of William Blake suspended from the ceiling with a leather belt fastened around his neck, his face distorted and blue in death.

Jesus Christ.

"Mr. Restrepo?"

Claudia Mercado's childlike voice brought me back to the here and now.

"Shadow and light?" I asked, recalling Claudia's ongoing struggle with perspective and light source.

Claudia nodded, gesturing toward the large sketch pad on her easel. "I'm not sure if the shadow is right."

I reached out and smudged her hard line of demarcation with a lump of kneaded eraser.

"Seeing the darkness is easy," I advised. "Seeing the light can be a bit of a challenge at times."

Later, my first session behind me, I was sipping Earl Gray tea and setting up the room for my afternoon class when a knock on the open door announced the surprise arrival of Duguay. He stood in the doorframe with a smile on his face and a potted phalaenopsis orchid in one hand. He'd exchanged his work uniform of crisp chinos and a polo for faded jeans and a light cotton pullover sweater. Duguay's hair, grown longer since I'd last seen him, was a wild, sexy mess that grazed his broad shoulders.

"Hello, stranger."

"Marc."

Duguay walked into the room and placed the plant on the center stand. I thanked him for the gift and moved to embrace him in friendly fashion, but Duguay took my hands, pulled me to him, and pressed his mouth to mine. I opened to him, heart pounding and almost dizzy with delight.

"I thought you said you'd wait until I started painting again," I said when we came up for air.

"I lied," Marc whispered, his lips brushing mine. "I couldn't wait for this any longer."

"Well, my next class starts in ten minutes. An hour and a half and I'm all yours."

"All mine?"

I gasped as he pressed his body close. "Nurse Practitioner, you seem to be suffering from a sudden onset of priapism. You need to get that seen to."

"That is my intention."

"An hour and a half."

"I'll hold you to it."

*

That evening, I lay—contented as a cat—curled up on Marc's sofa with my head nestled in his lap, his fingers toying with the strands of my hair.

"You're sure this isn't a mistake?" I asked.

"No. The professional part of me says it's too soon. My heart tells me it's now or never."

I sighed, grasped Marc's right hand and pulled it to my mouth, kissed it. "But it's perfect right now, isn't it?"

"Yes."

"I love monosyllabic responses. There's no arguing with them."

Marc laughed and wrapped his arms around my shoulders. "I'm hungry," he said.

"You're insatiable."

"Hungry for dinner."

"Well, you're aware of my culinary shortcomings. You can't expect me to do the romantic bit and whip up something fabulous from what I find in your refrigerator."

"Common ground, Cal. Nachos are my specialty—and I'm out of tortilla chips."

"Grubhub."

"Takes forty-five minutes, at least."

I pulled at the loose belt of my borrowed robe, teasing the garment from my body.

"Imagine what we can do in forty-five minutes."

"Hum. And my laptop *is* in my bedroom."

"No brainer."

"Yes."

*

It was a testament to the power of our mutual desire to get horizontal that Marc had failed to show me his garden the day before and that I'd barely noticed it. It surrounded his house, a beautifully designed oasis. There were no flowers. Everywhere were varying shades and textures of green in multicolored shrubs, trees, and plants. Pops of yellow, orange, and purple created a tapestry effect in the groundcover, through which a stream wended its way, emptying into a pond beneath a red pagoda.

"This is amazing," I said, wondering where Marc found the time for it.

"Believe it or not," replied Marc, anticipating my question, "it's fairly low maintenance. I'd love to take credit for it, but it was my father who designed and planted it. I told him I wanted my own world. This was the result."

"It's a true secret garden," I said, glancing up at the tall redwood-and-steel slipfence. "It feels as if there's no place beyond these boundaries."

"It's what I wanted...then."

"Now?"

"I still want that private world. But, I'm ready to share it."

"Like your love of the sea."

Marc inclined his head and sipped his coffee.

We sat at a bistro table under a canopy of poincianas, a French press and a small plate of baklava between us. The morning air was nippy, unusually so for late September, but with the warmth of Marc's company, the serenity of the garden, and the intimacy of our repast, it might have been the height of summer.

"How did you end up here?" I asked, reaching for a piece of sticky pastry.

"In this house? In Rowayton? Or in Connecticut in general?"

"All of the above."

"Well, I did my graduate work at Sacred Heart, in Fairfield. Malhotra's alma mater. She's the one who turned me on to POW, by the way. But that's another story. Anyway, my best friend at school, Trisha, was from Rowayton, and her parents adopted me as a sort of surrogate child. I spent a lot of time here and got to love the area. My parents bought me this house as a graduation present."

"Making up for Ernie and Bert?" I asked.

Marc laughed. "I admit it. I'm a spoiled brat. The classic only child." He poured more coffee for both of us, then asked, "What about you?"

It was an innocent question—and a natural one, since Marc had told me a good deal about his parents and his childhood in the course of everyday conversation, while I'd remained silent about my family and my youth.

"I'm not an only child," I replied, suddenly feeling the chill in the air, the enchantment of the moment broken. "I'm the only one left."

Marc didn't say anything. He reached under the table and gave one of my knees a gentle, reassuring squeeze. Better than words.

"My parents are both gone," I continued. "My mother died about three years ago, my father two years earlier. My father had cancer. For my mother, it was a stroke. It was hard losing them. Especially my mother. But they were elderly." I took a deep breath, pushing down the incipient anxiety.

"I didn't talk to Malhotra about my sister," I found myself admitting, eyes on the tabletop, examining the pattern of the tiles. "I pretended not to remember. But it all came back to me when Joshua brought me my photo albums."

I griped my mug with both hands and looked up at Marc. "Her name was Deanna. It happened when she and a bunch of her friends were in a van on their way to a sweet-sixteen party. They were all killed. Deanna was the only one who wasn't high."

Marc responded with a sharp intake of breath but continued to hold his tongue.

Moving my forefinger in circles on the table, I said, "I try to see a pattern, find a reason why Paul should have died in a similar way. There isn't one, of course. Fatal traffic accidents happen all the time. Still..." I shrugged and sipped at my coffee.

"Still," said Marc softly, "You want to know why. The unceasing thirst for answers is both a blessing and curse for us humans. Sometimes, it's incredibly difficult to accept that there may not be an answer, or, at least, one that we can understand."

"I know. Then, of course, there's the guilt. Survivor guilt. I think I've got my head around that one. Almost."

Liar.

Swish-thunk. Swish-thunk.

I love you.

"There's something else," said Marc, pulling me out of the rain and the dark and back into the peace of his garden. He reached across the small table and caressed the top of my hand, gently encouraging.

"Yes," I replied, turning my hand up to entwine my fingers with Marc's. "One of my students. A talented kid with great parents and a bright future ahead of him. He killed himself while I was in la-la land at Wending Hills. Declan told me. It's the worst unanswered 'why' of them all, Marc."

I told Marc about William Blake and found comfort in the telling. I also felt like Debbie Downer.

"Our first morning after and our conversation is about death."

"I'm glad that you trust me enough to open up like this," said Marc. "When you were my patient, I could tell you were holding a lot inside. Things you needed to come to terms with on your own time. I was conflicted, Cal. I wasn't 100 percent certain I was doing the right thing, that I might not be harming you by stepping away too soon. After a long talk with Dr. Malhotra, I decided I'd made the right choice."

"I was afraid I'd lose you," I said.

"There was never any danger of that. I was hooked from that first morning in your garden."

"And here we are in yours."

"Are you hooked?"

"Most definitely."

"Good. Then let's go back to bed."

*

Billy.

I'd always thought of him as William, and it felt odd, at first, using the diminutive. But as a friendship developed between the Blakes and me, and I began my work on their son's exhibit, it was impossible not to fall into the habit. He'd been Billy to his family and his artist signature was a stylized *BB*, so Billy it would be.

"His work is incredibly mature."

This appraisal came from Mahmood Nouri, Director of Graduate Studies in Painting at a well-respected local university. Mahmood was a one-time college classmate and occasional fellow partygoer on the fund-raising circuit. He'd been invaluable in helping me with my own exhibit, and I hoped he'd do the same for Billy's.

"Billy painted that when he was nine," I said, referring to the small seascape Mahmood was holding.

"Shit. No wonder Cooper snapped him up."

Mahmood returned the painting to my desk. It had been a special gift to me from Edward and Rhea Blake.

"It's such a shame," Mahmood continued. "Imagine what more he might have achieved...given time." He rubbed his short, gray beard. "But that's depressing speculation. What we have here is phenomenal."

Mahmood turned his attention to a collection of small, spiral-bound sketchbooks and notepads. Sitting cross-legged on the floor of my workroom, he sifted through the books, grunting, huffing, and occasionally making appreciative comments between sips of his vodka and cranberry juice.

"You know, Cal," Mahmood said. "Some of Billy's most interesting work is here, in these little books. The challenge is going to be how to display them to best effect...how to incorporate them into the collection of larger works." He held up a small Mead notebook, open to a pencil study. "Take a look at this."

I joined Mahmood on the floor and took the requested look. The sketch was a variation on one of Enlightenment artist William Blake's most famous works, the title of which escaped me. Mahmood provided it.

"*The Night of Enitharmon's Joy*," he said. "Billy's version. You know how important sexuality—sensuality—

was to William Blake's work, both written and illustrated. But there was a mysterious, almost frustrating coyness to much of it. This work always interested me for its blatantly masculinized depiction of the central female subject, Enitharmon, who in Blake's mythology represents the rule of the female will. The continual struggle between Enitharmon and her male counterpart, Los, for dominance is central to Blake's universe.

"But Billy, bless his heart, stripped away any nominal vestiges of femininity from Enitharmon simply by removing her flowing tresses and adding a beard.

With a couple tweaks, Billy has brought into question the assumed male-female duality in Blake's work and proposed a subtext of homosexuality. Brilliant!"

I made a mental note to research William Blake's work since I could see where Mahmood was going with this.

"You want to make the links—both obvious and subtle—between Billy and William Blake central to the exhibit," I said, shaking my head. "I don't like it. This is supposed to be about Billy."

"I didn't say 'central.' But to ignore them would be a mistake. William Blake's work informs so much of Billy's. The coincidence of their shared names might have been what drew Billy to Blake, but Billy clearly felt a deeper connection."

Mahmood rubbed his beard again, then tousled his head of curly salt-and-pepper hair until it stood on end.

"Look," he continued. "How about we find some way to use these notebooks as a link between the larger works? Maybe we can create a chronology in Billy's creative development. A notebook here, a painting there. Yes... I can an see it. Cal, if we can only—"

Mahmood stopped short when he realized I wasn't listening.

"Cal? What's wrong? You're not paying the least bit of attention."

I was looking at the small notebook that lay open on Mahmood's thigh.

I stared at Billy's sketch of Enitharmon with shaved head and beard and realized, as the room spun around me, that I was looking at a portrait of Paul.

*

"It does *look* like him," said Joshua doubtfully as he gazed at the photocopy of the drawing he held in one hand, while he gently stirred polenta with the other. "But Paul had that classic 'Roman bust' face, didn't he? Hawk nose, high cheekbones, stern mouth. Lots of Italian men *look* like Paul."

I turned the breaded pork cutlets to the other side, checking their color. Perfect. Joshua would berate me if they were otherwise. As I watched them sizzle and breathed in the aromas of hot oil, garlic, and rosemary, my thoughts were firmly on Paul. *Cotoletta di manzo* was one of his favorite dishes.

Joshua set down the paper and tasted his polenta. Then, he took a swig of wine and glanced back at the drawing of the ersatz Enitharmon. I saw his eyes narrowing, considering. Just as mine had done.

"Down to that little shadow in the earlobe?" I probed. "Where Paul's teenaged piercing had closed over?"

"Hmm. Well, they had met each other, right?"

I nodded. "A few times. At the center."

"There you have it, darling. Artists often use total strangers as subjects. So, it's no surprise that Billy might have used the likeness of his mentor's lover."

"*His mentor's lover.* The way you put that makes it sound even creepier that it already is."

"Creepy?"

"Odd, at least."

"What aren't you telling me?"

As I plated the cutlets, dressed them with gremolata, and handed the dishes to Joshua for the addition of the polenta, I related my memory of the coffee morning with Elspeth and her story of the lanky shape of Billy Blake loitering in my backyard.

"That sounds like—"

"Stalking?"

"No," said Joshua, making an annoyed face at my interruption. "I was going to say obsession or fixation."

"But why Paul?"

"You mean, why not you?"

"Exactly. Students develop crushes on their teachers—obsess over them sometimes, I imagine. But their teacher's lover?" I shook my head over something I considered highly improbable.

"Maybe Elspeth was confusing things," suggested Joshua as we tucked into our meal. "Didn't you tell me Billy used to hang out with Declan and look at his etchings or whatever? She probably mixed up your garden with hers."

"That's what I thought...then. But now, there's the portrait of Paul."

"Ergo, the creepy feeling." Joshua nodded as he sipped his Orvieto. "Still, it could be just the jumbled memories of an elderly woman with senile dementia and a perfectly innocent, if intriguing, choice of model by Billy."

I conceded the point. But it also occurred to me that I'd only assumed Billy had visited Declan's home. I remembered Billy expressing his admiration for Declan's stained-glass designs, but Declan could have brought them to the center to show Billy. In fact, it was much more likely.

We ate in the nook on mismatched plates with paper towels for napkins—a degree of informality which would have annoyed Paul but was a step above my recently acquired habit of eating on the living room sofa with my food on my lap, my tablet in one hand, and Bruno at my feet.

"Getting back to the land of the living," said Joshua as he served himself more polenta, "have you seen Marc again since your exchange of carnal knowledge?"

"Not yet. We have a date planned for Thursday."

"A *date*? That sounds so prim and proper."

"What else am I supposed to call it? We're going to see *Ghosts* at Yale Rep."

"Well, *that* will put you in the mood," said Joshua despairingly. "Only you would choose Ibsen for a romantic night out."

"It was Marc's idea, actually."

"You two really are made for each other, it would seem. Congratulations."

Joshua's delivery was typically sarcastic, but I knew him well enough to discern the underlying sincerity.

"Thank you."

A moment later, my cellphone trilled, and I nearly jumped out of my chair to go and answer the call, thinking of Marc.

Joshua laughed, then began a spirited rendition of Vikki Carr's "It Must be Him."

"Oh, shut up!"

I was laughing, too, as I made the demand, but Joshua was kind enough to switch to a low hum. By the time I retrieved my phone from my jacket hanging in the entry hall, the ringing had ceased.

Damn.

My disappointment was greater than I'd have liked to admit when I saw that the caller had not been Marc.

"Mahmood," I said, rejoining Joshua.

"Sorry, darling. I shouldn't have jinxed you with my serenade."

I waved away Joshua's apology as I read the text Mahmood had left.

"He says he's found something important in Billy's notebooks. He says we need to discuss it before proceeding with the exhibition."

"That sounds intentionally mysterious."

I shrugged. "You know Mahmood; he loves drama as much as you do."

"True."

"Whatever it is," I said, putting the phone aside, "it can wait until I see him later this week."

*

On my first of two trips to New Haven that week, I met Mahmood at his office on the university campus. It was a cozy room with a small fireplace, much original detail, and a view of the Peabody Museum through tall, narrow windows. The furniture was antique and notwithstanding the presence of the iMac, telephone and coffee maker, the room appeared to have remained essentially unchanged over hundreds of years. Dr. Mahmood Nouri, in jeans, T-shirt, and casual blazer, with small gold hoops in both ears, was perhaps the most anachronistic object in the room.

"Thanks for meeting me here, Cal," said Mahmood as he poured coffee into a mug and handed it to me. "I appreciate the inconvenience to you, not having your own wheels at the moment, but my schedule this week is insane."

"I'm becoming enamored with taxis and Uber," I replied, accepting the mug and taking a tentative sip. "Although my medical advisors say I'm perfectly fit to drive again, it's the psychological hurdle I'm having trouble with."

"These things take time," said Mahmood, his deep voice and slight Middle Eastern accent giving weight to the cliché phrase. "You're certainly looking well. I see you've divested yourself of the walking stick."

"Yes. It was becoming a crutch."

"Pun intended?"

"Oh—no, just poor word choice."

Mahmood laughed, then his expression quickly turned serious. He took a long drink of his coffee and regarded me with a keen look—as if he were judging the effect upon me of the words he had yet to speak.

Finally, he said, "Both you and Billy's parents have characterized the young man as something of a loner. But what I've seen and read thus far in Billy's sketchbooks and journals tells another story. There was at least one person with whom Billy had a lengthy and intense relationship."

"Well," I interjected, "there's a girl who, according to Mr. and Mrs. Blake, was very close with Billy growing up, and they remained so into high school. Mrs. Blake is under the impression that their relationship might have 'moved to the next level,' so to speak. But Mr. Blake disagrees. He thinks Billy was gay. My impression of Billy agrees with Mr. Blake's, but aside from Belinda—the old school friend—there doesn't seem to have been any significant other in Billy's life."

It sounded reasonable, convincing. But my mind kept pulling up that sketch of Paul. It *was* Paul. I knew it like I knew the sun would set in the evening. And I knew Billy had been to my house, and he had not come to see *me*. Yet, it was hardly an open-and-shut case, hardly proof of anything irregular. Then why had this stone of dread been lodged in the pit of my stomach for the last week?

"Interesting," said Mahmood, rubbing his beard. "My use of the term 'person' earlier sprang from a career-long adherence to PC phraseology; not from any vagary in Billy's work. Only a fraction of the art collection is overtly sexual in nature, but that small amount is unquestionably homoerotic—although it's nothing that would not have passed muster in old William Blake's time."

"Not Aubrey Beardsley material?"

"Heavens, no."

Mahmood topped up his coffee and raised the carafe in my direction with a questioning look.

"No, thanks. I've barely touched mine."

Mahmood was one of those people who took pleasure in scalding hot beverages and pizza straight from the oven.

"Billy's written work," continued Mahmood, settling his ample buttocks once more into his leather chair, "is a horse of an entirely different color."

"Oh?"

"I'm not a blushing virgin, but I have to admit I was shocked at the explicitness of Billy's writing. Much of it borders on pornography."

And I'll bet you got off reading it, didn't you?

The inappropriate, snide comment didn't pass my lips, but Mahmood must have read it in my eyes because he squirmed a little before he continued.

"I assumed it was mostly fantasy. The frustrated yearnings of a horny, lonely teenager."

"Hardly shocking, Mahmood," I countered. "Even if Billy were inexperienced, he'd not likely have been ignorant. The internet doesn't leave much to a kid's imagination these days."

"True. The young man's sexual flights of fancy alone would not have raised a red flag. It was the letters."

"Letters?"

"Um-hum."

Mahmood nodded vigorously as he drank more java. "From Billy to someone he called Enitharmon...and from this Enitharmon to Billy."

"You mean he—he invented a relationship? Wrote and received correspondence from an imaginary person?"

I wondered if my need for this assumption to be true was revealed in the tone of my voice, the slight tremble, the stutter.

"Not at all. I believe Enitharmon was quite real."

Mahmood fished a set of keys from his jeans and proceeded to open a file drawer in his desk. I recognized at once that the small bundle Mahmood took from the drawer was a portion of Billy's notebooks.

"I suppose you can't properly call them letters," Mahmood said, pulling off the rubber band that held the notebooks together. "I mean, they're not postmarked. Love notes would be a better name for them. Since Billy possessed both those he wrote and many of those written by Enitharmon, I would conjecture that it was some romantic exercise, some sort of role-playing fantasy—obviously one inspired by William Blake, as Billy refers to himself as Los."

Mahmood opened one of the spiral notebooks and removed a folded sheet of white stationary. He cleared his throat and proceeded to read aloud.

My Enitharmon,

The waiting is becoming unbearable.

When shall we become as one?

Again, and again, you've told me we must wait— that I must wait.

That the time is not right.

That I am not ready.

That you are not prepared to commit.

You said that the world was not prepared to accept our union...not yet.

Not yet.

How I've come to despise those words.

I need you so much.

I'm being childish, I know.

What is another month after all this time?

Forgive me.

I await you.

Your Los.

"This is the last of the notes from Billy to Enitharmon," said Mahmood, refolding the paper and placing it in the notebook. "The last that I know of anyway. They go back nearly two years. Interestingly, those written from Enitharmon to Billy are much less flowery...more down to earth, practical. It seems clear to me, from a close reading of these notes, that Enitharmon was older, more experienced. There are numerous references to 'waiting.' Waiting for Enitharmon to be free, waiting for Billy—or Los—to be of legal age—"

"What?"

"As I said, some of this correspondence dates to when Billy would have been around sixteen or seventeen. It seems Billy was eager to take the relationship 'to the next level,' to use your phrase. But Enitharmon was adamant about keeping things platonic until Billy reached his maturity."

"*Reached his maturity*? You make it sound almost Victorian."

"That's how Enitharmon comes across, I guess," replied Mahmood. "I mean, I applaud his decision not to enter into a sexual relationship with a minor, but his tone is…I don't know. Sanctimonious? Yes, that's the right word. Sanctimonious. At least in the later notes. The early ones are a bit more…erm…earthy. But as far as I can understand, much of this 'relationship' never went beyond paper. The whole thing is weird."

I suppose it was morbid curiosity that prompted my next question.

"Do you have one of Enitharmon's notes?" I tried to put on a face of puzzled inquisitiveness—as if I found this as "beyond weird" as did Mahmood. Nothing to do with me.

"Yes. Here; take a look at this one."

Mahmood handed me a piece of folded stationary. Heavier than the other. Good quality.

I know that paper…

I only pretended to read the brief note. It didn't matter what it said. The handwriting alone said enough. The same elaborate, calligraphic script Paul had used for dinner party invitations. There had been enough of them over the years. Paul's hand...Paul's words.

Suddenly, the cozy room felt cloyingly close. I experienced the same queer tilting sensation that had overcome me that day at Balducci's when Belinda had confronted me about what I thought was my affair with Eric. With a nauseating flash of clarity, I replayed her words in an entirely different context.

"You could have done something to stop it, but you didn't."

She hadn't been talking about me and her father. She hadn't known.

She'd been talking about Paul and Billy.

Jesus Christ...

"Cal?"

Mahmood's voice came to me from some other plane of existence. From the world where things were still normal. Still right.

"Cal, are you okay? You look green at the gills."

"Huh? Oh...I think it's the heat. The fireplace, the coffee. I don't know. I'm still not 100 percent."

"You're right, it is stuffy. Let's get some air in here."

As Mahmood worked the crank mechanism on one of the windows, he continued to explore the possible significance of Billy's notes.

"Two things strike me about the note I just read aloud," he said. "There are dates on all of Billy's notes, so it's not difficult to establish a chronology. The one I read was written just two weeks before Billy's suicide. Does anything in that note sound to you like something written by someone intending to take his own life?"

I shook my head, still feeling hot despite the cool air now flowing into the room.

"No," agreed Mahmood, resuming his position behind his desk. "That's romantic hyperbole written by an imaginative teenager in love. There's yearning in those words, not despair."

"What's the second thing?"

"There's no reply."

I considered that for a moment, turning Paul's note over on my lap so the truth was facing the other way.

"What?" I asked. "Are you saying you think Billy's lover dumped him? That that's what led to his suicide?"

"It's the first thing that came to my mind. But it doesn't fit with what we can glean from Enitharmon's side of the correspondence. An abrupt and complete volte-face seems unlikely."

Mahmood looked at the note that lay in my lap and then up at me.

"Another possibility is that Enitharmon passed away," Mahmood added softly. His voice was low, considering, as he continued. "If my assumption is correct and Enitharmon was considerably older than Billy, this scenario seems much more likely. A heart attack...an accident?" Mahmood shrugged. "Who knows?"

"Yes," I agreed, folding the note and passing it to Mahmood across his desk. "That's definitely a possibility." Did he note the tremor in my hand as he accepted it?

"Odd thing about this note," said Mahmood, replacing the missive in the spiral notebook, "is that I can't help but feel there's something familiar about it. About all Enitharmon's notes, for that matter. The tone of voice maybe? Or the handwriting..."

Of course.

In my mind's eye I could see Paul writing those dinner invitations, addressing the envelopes. Dr. Mahmood Nouri had been a frequent guest at those parties.

He knows.

He saw Paul's face in that sketch, just as I had.

And now, the notes.

I didn't trust my voice—what words it might form in reply. I simply stared at the notebook, licked my parched lips. When I finally looked up at Mahmood, I saw not accusation but gentle kindness in his brown eyes.

"We'll never know the entire truth, Cal," he said softly. "Maybe your earlier idea is correct. Maybe Enitharmon only existed in Billy's head. Maybe Billy was the hand behind Enitharmon's notes. Billy was, after all, a very gifted artist."

At last, I spoke.

"I'll always know the truth, Mahmood," I said, my voice hardly more than a whisper.

I contemplated the floor as I listened to Mahmood open and close a drawer in his desk. The clink of glass and the squeak and pop of a decanter being opened pulled my gaze away from the carpet and back to my friend.

"For medicinal purposes," said Mahmood as he poured, and the delicate scent of fine cognac made its way to my nostrils.

I accepted the heavy crystal tumbler, certain Mahmood understood my gratitude extended beyond that for the welcome shot of alcohol.

"We'll have to rethink my idea for the exhibit, of course," Mahmood said after we'd sipped in silence for a moment. "Most of Billy's writing is much too personal to be on public display. But the general premise should still work." Mahmood traced a finger over the surface of the spiral notebook. "Billy's parents handed these books over to you sight unseen, am I correct?"

I nodded.

"Then perhaps they should remain unseen by the Blakes. Not everything, of course. But, with careful editing, they need not know that a few items went astray." Mahmood looked toward the small fireplace. "Sometimes the old school methods work the best."

"No."

Mahmood raised his thick eyebrows in surprise.

"There's someone who needs to see them first," I continued. "Someone who has the right. Someone who, I think, loved Billy very much."

*

Arranging a meeting with Belinda Lindstrom might have proved an easier said than done proposition. For reasons that were now becoming clear to me, Belinda and I had never been on friendly—or even neighborly—terms. Openly seeking her out for a heart-to-heart talk was not an option. Subtler means were needed. I considered that, if I'd had a car at my disposal, I could have employed the old trick of tailing her, conniving a faux impromptu fancy-meeting-you-here moment. In the end, no Secret Squirrel antics were necessary. The meeting practically arranged itself.

"Not bad."

The words were delivered with the considered intonation of a connoisseur. Susan took another bite and examined the chocolate chip cookie over the top of her glasses. Pushing the spectacles back up the bridge of her nose, she continued her critique.

"Much better than my mom's Nestle's Toll House. This is the real thing."

I smiled at her compliment and at the ludicrous Minnie Mouse ears into which she'd screwed her curly blond hair. Fortunately, she hadn't yet asked me if I liked them.

"Thank you," I replied as I turned the handle of the molinillo between my palms. Chocolate was something I really did know how to make. One of the few practical things I'd learned from my father. "But compliments should go to Mrs. Mac Graith. It's her recipe."

"If you can master her poppy seed cake," said Susan, "I might just move in."

Heart wrenching words. I thought of Eric and his fantastic plans for a future with me and his daughter as a family unit.

Had they really been that fantastic? In the cozy confines of my kitchen, with Susan chomping happily on cookies and the aroma of chocolate filling the room, they didn't seem fantastic at all...

"Can we have marshmallows on top?" Susan asked as she ambled over to inspect the chocolate pot. Bruno rose from his snooze beneath the table in the nook and trotted expectantly behind her.

"Marshmallows?" I demanded with exaggerated outrage. "My dear girl, one does not ruin good chocolate with marshmallows. That's a gringo abomination."

"Isn't gringo a racist slur?"

Susan's eyes were wide and innocent behind her eyeglasses, but I noted the slight sarcastic twitch to her mouth.

"Disparaging, not racist."

Susan considered my avoidance tactic for a moment with furrowed brow, then shrugged her shoulders in defeat. "Is it ready?"

"Just about. Get two mugs from the cupboard."

There were only two mugs independent of a set: the Paris mug and one decorated with Christmas trees. Susan chose these, commenting on their cuteness.

"I have no idea where this came from," I said, accepting the Christmas one. "Probably my mother. She had a thing for yuletide paraphernalia."

"And this one?" asked Susan as I poured her chocolate into the Paris mug. I hesitated, then decided to tell her the whole story—well, most of it—as the chocolate cooled.

"Wow," Susan said when my tale had come to an end. "That's *so* romantic."

I smiled and encouraged Susan to try her chocolate. This elicited another "wow."

"I thought the cloves would make it taste gross," she admitted, "but this is epic!"

We sipped the fragrant beverage, dunked our cookies, and munched in contented silence for a while before Susan said, "You must really miss Paul. Belinda was a wreck when her friend Billy died. She didn't *show* it; you know what I mean? She always tries to act so sophisticated. But I heard her crying sometimes. Billy was one of your students, right?"

Tread carefully, Calixto.

"I didn't know Billy and Belinda were close."

"BFFs. Mom thought he was weird, so he hardly ever came to our house. Belinda always went to his place. The Blakes are awesome."

I had to agree. "Ed and Rhea have asked me to curate an exhibit of Billy's work."

"Really? That will make Belinda *so* happy."

A perfect segue if ever there was one.

"Do you think Belinda would like to help me?" I asked. "Since she and Billy were such good friends, she might be able to give me some ideas...some insight."

Susan nodded vigorously. "She'd love it."

"I'm not exactly Belinda's favorite person," I said doubtfully.

Susan made a dismissive gesture with her free hand. "Leave her to me."

I had to remind myself that I was talking to an eleven-year-old.

*

Belinda agreed to meet me at the center. I had no classes on Thursdays, but when I informed Melody of the ostensible purpose of my interview with Billy's friend, she allowed me the use of the art room.

"I've never been here before," said Belinda as she entered the room. "But Billy described it so well that it feels familiar."

I turned away from the sketch of Marc's garden I'd been working on as a framework for a watercolor study and faced Eric's elder daughter. She appeared mature beyond her years in a tailored gray suit, with her hair swept into a chignon like that favored by her mother. The resemblance between mother and daughter was striking.

"Job interview?" I guessed.

"Internship. A law firm in Milford. It's part of my freshman year work-study program."

Belinda did not elaborate further. She shed her blazer and made a circuit of the room, high heels clicking on the parquet.

"What was Billy's favorite place?" she asked.

I shrugged. "Anywhere. I encourage students to change places frequently. But he did have a favorite easel."

"He told me," said Belinda, a smile softening her features, conjuring shades of Eric rather than Jill. "Which one?"

I stepped back from my work in progress.

"This one. I know it may sound silly, but I thought it might inspire me—that maybe something of Billy's spirit was still in it...part of it."

"That doesn't sound silly at all," said Belinda as she put a hand to the wooden frame. "And your sketch is beautiful. Billy admired your work so much. And he admired *you*. Sometimes, I felt sure he was in love with you."

The tears came suddenly, stripping away Belinda's veneer of sophistication and maturity. Raw grief, no doubt hitherto held under tight wraps, had made her a child again. I moved to embrace her and was surprised to find her return the gesture in kind, leaning her face down to press into my hair. She cried softly for a while, then pulled away.

"I'm sorry."

Unsure what she was apologizing for, I simply shook my head to negate the sentiment. "Would you like some tea?"

Belinda sniffled and nodded.

I nuked two mugs of hot water and added a sachet of Earl Gray to each.

"That smells good."

"Honey?"

Another nod. "My grandmother got me into tea," Belinda elaborated as she accepted her mug. "Earl Gray is one of my favorites."

"Mine too."

Ice having been broken, we sipped in silence for a while, then Belinda said, "I'm sorry for the way I talked to you that day at Balducci's. I was just so angry."

She looked around the room, her gaze unfocused.

"It's weird," Belinda continued, "how you think you know someone, but you really don't. Not everything."

"That's what you said to me that day," I said. "You said 'you don't know me.'"

"Yeah. I guess I was thinking of me and Billy. When we were younger, I was in denial about Billy being gay. I mean, everyone called Billy gay. But they didn't *know*. 'Gay' is what some kids call anyone who's different—who doesn't fit in, who doesn't think and act the way they're *supposed* to. 'You're so gay' is like one of the worst insults a guy can receive—and there doesn't have to be any basis in fact."

"Apparently, things haven't changed that much since I was a kid."

Belinda shrugged. It was a world-weary gesture, and it saddened me that someone so young should have given up so soon.

"Anyway," continued Belinda, "I just thought Billy was different, at first. And he was. It was like—like he came from some other planet and he was learning how to be human. They taught us about autism in a forum once, and I wondered if Billy was on the spectrum. His parents never mentioned it, and I think they would have if they knew. So, I did my own research and decided he wasn't. He was just Billy."

I thought of what Declan had said about people wearing masks, being chameleons in order to survive. I related Declan's views on Billy, and life in general, and Belinda surprised me by shaking her head.

"I get your friend's point, but that wasn't Billy. Part of his differentness was that he was so open emotionally.

Like that old saying goes, he wore his heart on his sleeve. I don't understand why Billy did what he did, but that's my own fault."

"How do you figure?"

"The last few months before Billy died, we didn't see much of each other. I spent a lot of time at my grandparents' house—my grandfather was in the hospital and my grandmother needed company—and Billy was caught up in plans for his move to New York. That's what I assumed anyway. If I'd spent more time with him, listened more closely to what he was saying, I would have understood what was really going on."

"I said as much to Declan about myself," I admitted. "And Billy's parents have said the same to me. But we can't blame ourselves, Belinda. Everyone has secrets. Everyone has parts of themselves that they don't share with anyone else, no matter how close they might be to another person."

"I know you're right," Belinda mumbled into her mug. "It's just going to take me a while to accept it."

I refreshed our tea. Then, as I removed some of Billy's notebooks and sketchpads from a shopping bag, I asked the big question.

"When did you find out about Paul?"

Belinda stood and joined me at the card table where I'd laid out Billy's things next to the microwave. She cradled her mug to her chest and stared at the table as she spoke.

"Billy called him Enitharmon. I wasn't entirely sure he was a real person until pretty recently," she began. "Billy told me last year that he and this guy were planning a future together, but he wouldn't tell me who he was. Billy was uncharacteristically cagey with me, and I still thought maybe he was making it all up. Maybe that's what I wanted to believe. When I pressed him, Billy admitted he couldn't reveal the guy's name because he was older. Way older. He said he'd tell me everything once we graduated and everything was "set."

"I thought it was weird, but Bill was so happy, so excited. And, well, I'd heard of students—girls—marrying teachers right after graduation. In fact, one of the seniors last year married her chemistry teacher. So, I figured, why should it be different for a gay guy?"

"You believed Enitharmon was one of your teachers?"

This elicited a guffaw from Belinda. "The only possible candidate would have been Mr. Lowenstein, our English lit instructor. He's about a hundred years old and looks like Mr. Burns from the Simpsons."

Belinda gave a dramatic shudder, and I couldn't help but smile.

"Actually," continued Belinda, "at first, I thought it was you."

My smile faded.

"He was infatuated with you, Cal. It was obvious. And totally understandable. I mean, like, if Pique or Cristiano Ronaldo had come to coach my soccer team. I get it. He admired your talent, and you're hot. For an older guy."

"Um...thanks."

"You know what I mean. But Enitharmon was different. Billy was in love. I decided that if Billy wouldn't tell me who this guy was, I'd find out on my own. I'm not proud of what I did, but I had to know."

Belinda pointed to the array of Billy's work. "I went to meet Billy one day at his house and purposely showed up early—before I knew he'd be home. Mrs. Blake trusted me like I was her own kid. I went up to Billy's room to wait for him, and I..."

"Went through his stuff."

"Yeah. I said I wasn't proud. Anyway, that's when I found this weird sketch."

"*The Night of Enitharmon's Joy*," I said, picking up the blue Mead notebook. "Billy's version."

Belinda eyed the notebook and then looked up at me with a sad half-smile.

"You, too, huh?"

"Yes. I had no idea Paul was involved with Billy until I saw it. There are letters, also. They're what convinced me. Paul's handwriting...his style."

"I apologize, Cal. For thinking the worst of you."

It was my turn for the world-weary shrug.

"They say the spouse always knows," I said. "But I was clueless."

I nearly told Belinda about Paul's decision to join the Church but checked myself as it dawned upon me that Paul's choice might have caused the end of his relationship with Billy—just as it had ended Paul's relationship with me. And it may well have been the catalyst for Billy's downward spiral, Paul's sudden death being the final tipping point. So, I kept my thoughts and mixed metaphors to myself. Instead, I posed the question that got to the point of my interview with Belinda. Her knowledge of the Enitharmon sketch made it much easier.

"How much of Billy's personal stuff have you read?"

If Belinda found the question rude or inappropriate, she didn't show it.

"Just that blue book," she said. "It was enough. Enough for what I wanted to know."

I sighed as I sat on the edge of the table. "The thing is, Billy's private world is nearly inextricable from his artwork—as is the case with many great artists. Billy can't tell me how much of that private world he would want revealed to the public. But I want this exhibit to show people who Billy was as much as show them the things he created—it's what Mr. and Mrs. Blake want."

I gestured toward the shopping bag. "That's all Billy's personal stuff—notebooks, sketches, letters. The Blakes entrusted everything to me, but you loved him, Belinda. Help me sort it out. Help me build a portrait of Billy for the world."

Belinda looked at me with eyes glistening with imminent tears, but a joyful smile lit up her face.

"Thank you, Cal," she said. "Let's do Billy proud."

Chapter Eleven

MARC

It would be an exaggeration to say that I felt bereft when I awoke alone on the morning following my first night and day of intimacy with Cal. But I noted the absence of him with a wistful pang. I've tried, since then, to avoid romantic projections: Cal at family gatherings, Cal and I adopting a dog or a cat, Cal and I choosing stationery for our wedding announcements. But it's impossible not to dream of such things when the circumstances that brought us together had been so benevolently guided by fate.

With time to spare before my first appointment of the day, I poured my third cup of coffee and took it into the living room. Slumping down in my sofa, I surveyed the wall facing me. Outfitted with long, wooden ceiling-to-floor shelves, the wall showcased my collection of books, many of which I'd retained since childhood. Early on in my residency at the cottage, I'd attempted to organize the books by theme—mystery, religion, history, etc.—but I'd ended up settling for arrangement by size and color, regardless of subject.

So much for my ex-lover's claim that I was anal-retentive.

I was neat. I was fastidious.

These traits did not necessarily indicate a personality disorder.

This is what I told myself as I rose and approached the bookcase, checking the alignment of book spines and checking for signs of nonexistent dust.

The contents of the center shelf were perfectly symmetrical in their arrangement, each the exact size and thickness of its predecessor or antecedent. Playbills. A collection going back to the seventies—the older issues handed down to me from my parents, those from the early nineties onward, a history of my personal experience with theater.

I could have found it blindfolded, so often had I pulled it out and poured over it during the preceding weeks. But I convinced myself that I was once more coming across it by chance. We lie to ourselves day in and day out. We rework the truth into something we can live with. Make it our own truth, our own reality. I opened the Playbill and read the title and credits:

Music by Kurt Weill

Lyrics by Ira Gershwin

Produced and Directed by Jim Campbell

With Millicent Kitay as Liza Elliot and Richard North as Russell Paxton

Costumes by Calixto Restrepo

Millicent Kitay had been my father's high school sweetheart. They'd maintained a long-distance friendship over the years since then, and it was on the strength of this friendship that my parents and I were invited as special guests to the opening night of a revival of *Lady in the Dark*.

After the curtain, I was introduced to the cast and to the show's costume designer and his boyfriend, pals of the leading man. I wouldn't remember any of the actors, or the boyfriend's name—or even what he looked like. But I would never forget Cal. I would never forget his exotic looks, his incredibly black eyes or the way he winked and said, "Pleased to meet you, handsome," when he shook my hand. The other adults laughed good-naturedly, taking the comment as a kindness, a way of making me feel less awkward, a condescension, really. But Cal's eyes said something else. They said that they saw past the acne, the glasses, and the bad haircut. They saw into me, into the adolescent yearning, into the need to belong.

The enchantment continued after the show as we all dined in a trendy restaurant in Chelsea. I sat between Cal and Millicent—between a Broadway legend and my first adult crush—and I felt I'd gone to heaven, or, as my dad would say, happy as a pig in shit. There I was, just for that moment in time, no longer a nerdy, queer nobody from a nowhere suburb of Chicago, but *somebody*. Somebody having dinner at the gay epicenter of Manhattan. Somebody pretending to understand the double entendres and the barbed compliments—and sometimes guessing right and feeling a rush of heat when Cal flashed one of his knowing smiles. Cal made me feel part of everything, as if we were both kids watching the adults get drunk and make fools of themselves.

I got drunk that night too. Drunk on possibilities. The next day on the train ride home, I looked at my reflection in the window, and I didn't see the pimples or the squinting eyes. I saw what I might be, what I could be. What I wanted to be. And for the first time, I thought there really might be a life worth living beyond the seventh grade. Cal's wink, Cal's smile had given me hope. He would not remember me, I was sure. But Calixto Restrepo had saved my life.

*

Last night, as Cal and I dined in a small, noisy, brick-oven pizzeria full of fellow theatergoers and a few of the actors from Yale Rep, I was reminded of that dinner so many years ago. I nearly told him. Nearly revealed my adolescent crush and how that chance meeting with a younger Cal had had such a profound influence on my life.

Nearly.

But something held me back. Maybe it was the fact that deep down somewhere, I was disappointed Cal had not remembered me. Though, realistically, rationally, I acknowledged that the possibility was highly unlikely. I was hardly recognizable now as the skinny, awkward, acne-cursed boy with horn-rimmed glasses and bad hair that I'd been at twelve. Cal, on the other hand, had changed little. A few gray hairs, a bit more weight. But his eyes, his smile, his laugh remained the same.

"Where are you, Nurse Practitioner?" Cal asked, tapping the top of my hand.

I turned my gaze away from the nearby table of actors and back into the present.

"Sorry. I was thinking of when my parents were still in the business. How they dragged me to so many shows. This kind of atmosphere takes me back."

"Me too. Though it's a bit more immediate in my case. You know, I feel nostalgic, but I don't really miss that world. I'm getting to love the world I'm in now. The strange thing is that I've got Paul to thank for it. If he hadn't taken that job in Stamford, I wouldn't be sitting here with you in this moment. I never seriously considered fate and coincidence as guiding forces in my life. Obviously, I've been wrong."

"Chance would be a fine thing," I murmured, and took a pull on my Peroni.

"What the heck does that mean, actually?" asked Cal. "I've heard the expression before but never understood it."

"Supposedly, it's first use dates to the nineteenth century. The English equivalent of 'fat chance.' A way to express doubt that something desired will actually come to pass. I misunderstood it for years. I thought it meant that it would be great if the Fates stepped in and worked their magic. I figured it was a wistful, hopeful phrase, not a sarcastic one. A Brit I knew in college set me straight, but I still cling to my own interpretation."

Cal devoured a square of thin, crisp pizza laden with prosciutto di Parma and arugula, nodding as he did so.

"I like hopeful," he said, wiping his mouth with his napkin. "I don't know if I did before—in my other life—but I do now."

I considered this, topping up Cal's glass of Cabernet.

"Do you think of your past that way?" I asked. "Another life?"

"Yeah. I think I have to. Malhotra was right. In some way, I've got a second chance—a fresh start. She said I should see my condition as a unique opportunity, not a disability. I thought she was full of shit then. But now...it makes sense. People often talk about starting over, quitting their job, moving away, reinventing themselves. But it's usually easier said than done. I think I've been given a gift, and I don't intend to squander it."

I love you.

The words didn't pass my lips, but their meaning must have shown in my eyes as I reached out and cupped Cal's free hand in my own.

"I love you too," he said.

Chance was, indeed, a fine thing.

Epilogue

CAL

I never did return to sleep in my old bedroom.

It's empty now. Everything that would have reminded me of my life with Paul is gone.

I stand there now, looking at the empty space, wondering how something—someone—can be there one day and gone the next.

I pick up the last of my plastic moving boxes.

I peer into the box.

It's in there, somewhere. The article. Printed out in the library at Wending Hills.

How did the story stick in my mind?

How did it resonate at that one crucial moment?

If the thought hadn't come to me, just in that tiny flash, would I be standing here now in an empty room, house sold, Marc waiting for me in his little cottage with its enchanted garden?

Chance would be a fine thing...

Yet another interpretation.

I set the box down, remove the lid, and root around until I find the red paper file folder.

The Lamarck Courier

September 22, 2011

Lamarck, West Virginia—A West Virginia woman who drove her sport utility vehicle off a cliff and into a lake in a crash last year that killed her and her two young children did so deliberately, officials said Wednesday.

The June 05, 2010, deaths were ruled a double homicide-suicide by the Brandywine County Coroner's Office, the office revealed in a statement.

Officials said thirty-eight-year-old Karen Downes drove a Kia Sportage off a sixty-foot cliff with her two sons inside. The vehicle sank in fifty feet of water in McCarthy Lake.

The bodies of Downes and eleven-year-old Guy Downes and eight-year-old Jeremy Downes were recovered, and the damaged vehicle was pulled from the lake.

The cause of death for all three was drowning associated with blunt force trauma.

Witnesses told investigators that Downes was driving on a state highway when she turned off and pointed the car toward the cliff, then suddenly accelerated.

Officials said they found nothing mechanically wrong with the vehicle.

The Brandywine County Sheriff's Office confirmed that forensic investigators concluded the evidence indicated Downes acted deliberately. Toxicology tests found no drugs or alcohol in Downes's system.

The sheriff's office declined to comment on Downes's motive.

I fold the photocopy and place it back in the folder, recalling Dr. Malhotra's prediction that I might see my past in a new light, look back on it as if I were viewing an unbiased biography.

She was right.

The clarity haunts me.

One moment. One mad thought—dismissed almost immediately.

But not soon enough.

Pelting rain.

The swish-thunk of the windshield wipers.

"How many ways can I say I'm sorry, Cal?" Paul demands, his words slurred slightly by liquor.

Paul, drunk. A first.

No response from me.

Swish-thunk.

"Cal, please. You know our relationship was over a long time ago."

"And whose fault is that?"

"Don't assign blame," says Paul, the word "assign" sounding more like "a shine."

"Don't talk like a fucking shrink."

Swish-thunk.

"Well, you know what one sounds like better than I."

Even drunk, Paul's grammar is irritatingly correct.

"That was low."

God, why did I ever tell Paul about that one-week fling with a psychiatrist?

"I'm sor—"

"Oh, for Christ's sake, Paul, stop it!"

Swish-thunk, swish-thunk, swish-thunk.

Paul's hand on my shoulder; his inebriated state allowing all his weight to lay into the gesture.

The car swerves.

How easy it would be to end it all. I think of that mother and her children I'd read about...everything over in minutes.

I pull myself back from the abyss at the sound of Paul's voice.

"You're crying," says Paul, his voice now piteous, like a small child concerned for his mother. A click as Paul unfastens his seatbelt and moves closer.

"No, I'm not. Get off me, Paul. I'm driving. Put your seatbelt back on."

I glance into the rearview mirror. A BMW that has been weaving in and out of lanes at speed is on top of me.

"Shit."

I try to slow down, to put some space between myself and the semi in front of me.

Impossible.

BMW feints a lane change.

Paul is pawing me, petting me.

Swish-thunk.

Swish-thunk.

"I love you, Cal."

Swish-thunk.

About Zev de Valera

Born in New York City and raised in the San Joaquin Valley of California, Zev now divides his time between Brooklyn, NY and Stratford, CT, where he lives with his husband, two cats, and two dogs.

Zev began writing when he was a child, scribbling observations of relatives and neighbors in a Mead notebook while the adults paid him no mind, and all the time devouring the works of Agatha Christie, Edgar Allan Poe, Jules Verne, and Phyllis A. Whitney.

Although Zev's future career path would lead him far afield from fiction writing, Zev continued to scribble and—many years later—found himself a published author.

Email

zevdevalera@outlook.com

Also from NineStar Press

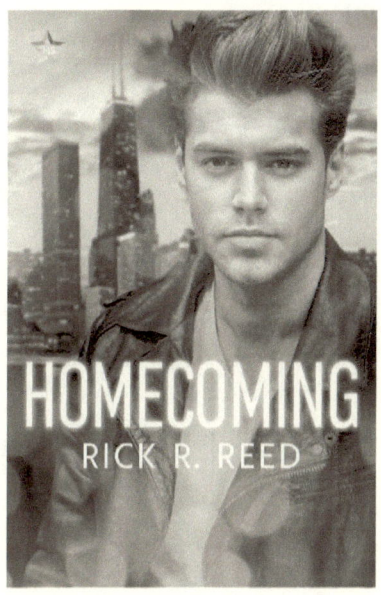

Homecoming by Rick R. Reed

After losing his partner Toby, Chase faces a long, painful road back to life and love.

At first, he doesn't see how he can go on, but then Chase and Toby's old friend Mike cajoles him into returning to Chicago for the annual International Mr. Leather Competition. There Chase revisits a world of hot, casual sex that he had forgotten existed, meets a friend who cares more for him than he ever realized, and discovers the possibility that he just might be able to move on without betraying the memory of his late partner.

Will Chase find his way back once more to life? To love? And will he find that place he's been missing? *Home.* You'll have to experience the heartrending journey firsthand to find out.

The Silence of Lightning by Marie S. Crosswell

Former pro-rodeo champion Smith Rose and his cousins Cooper and Christa Boone live a quiet life together in the town of Cody, Wyoming—until the summer of 2015 shakes them to their foundations.

Stuck in an unhappy rut since his retirement from the rodeo five years prior, Smith is forced to reckon with his past, present, and future when his former friend and lover John Henry Walker shows up at Smith's bar. Meanwhile, the Boone sisters face a threat they never would've predicted when an out-of-town stranger begins to stalk Christa after meeting her at a party. While trying to support her sister and their cousin, Cooper secretly agonizes over her fears of their little family splitting apart and where that would leave her.

When Smith, Cooper, and Christa's problems converge in a dangerous confrontation, will the three of them survive?

The Boss by J. Calamy

Nicholas Erickson is happy to be the smallest cog at the US Embassy in Singapore, a big step up from prison. Nick lives with a terrible secret: he killed a family of three in a traffic accident, for which he was imprisoned and became a pariah back home. The only threat to his second chance is the truth—and Nelson Graves.

Shipping Magnate Lord Nelson Graves is secretly the head of crime syndicate Red Sky, making him the biggest arms dealer and drug boss in Southeast Asia. Graves is tired, lonely, addicted to opium, and trying to get his imploding crime syndicate back to business. There is a traitor in his organization and an old enemy is back on his tail.

A romance builds between hot-headed, reckless Nick and unhappy, ruthless Graves. But nothing is that easy. Shoot-outs, bombings, and vindictive exes prove Nick's past and Graves's present may be a lethal combination.

Connect with NineStar Press

www.ninestarpress.com

www.facebook.com/ninestarpress

www.facebook.com/groups/NineStarNiche

www.twitter.com/ninestarpress

www.instagram.com/ninestarpress